GLORY DAYS

Also by Simon Rich

GLORY DAYS

Stories

SIMON RICH

Little, Brown and Company

New York   Boston   London

Copyright © 2024 by Simon Rich

Little, Brown and Company
Hachette Book Group
1290 Avenue of the Americas, New York, NY 10104
littlebrown.com

First Edition: July 2024

Little, Brown and Company is a division of Hachette Book Group, Inc. The Little, Brown name and logo are trademarks of Hachette Book Group, Inc.

The publisher is not responsible for websites (or their content) that are not owned by the publisher.

The Hachette Speakers Bureau provides a wide range of authors for speaking events. To find out more, go to hachettespeakersbureau.com or email hachettespeakers@hbgusa.com.

Little, Brown and Company books may be purchased in bulk for business, educational, or promotional use. For information, please contact your local bookseller or the Hachette Book Group Special Markets Department at special.markets@hbgusa.com.

"History Report," "Mario," "Millennial Fable," "Participation Trophy," "Punishment," and "Thanksgiving Rider" previously appeared in *The New Yorker*.

ISBN 9780316569002
LCCN 2024932746

Printing 1, 2024

LSC-C

Printed in the United States of America

For my wife and children

CONTENTS

CONTENTS

I

HISTORY REPORT

I interviewed my great-grandfather Simon because he is the oldest person in my family who is still alive. He was born in a country called America, on Earth. He said he used to be a writer. I asked him if he wrote *Spider-Man* and he said no, he wrote other things that have all been lost.

My great-grandfather was one of the only men to escape from Earth. The rest of the people who got seats on the Escape Pod were women and children. My great-grandfather says they let him on because "they needed one man to row the spaceship." I'm not sure what he means, because there are no oars on a spaceship, but that is what he said.

My great-grandfather told me how scary it was when Earth became too hot to live on. The skies burned with fire day and night, and you couldn't walk across the street without collapsing. I asked him if he had had any kind of warning about climate change and he said yes, there'd been articles, movies, and books about how it was going to happen. I asked him if he tried to stop it from happening and he said yes, of course. I asked him how and he said that he had done something called recycling, which is where you throw your garbage into different-colored boxes. I asked my mom what he was talking about, and she explained that when people become as old as my great-grandfather, their brains start to break down and it is almost like they turn back into babies.

Since my great-grandfather is going to die soon, and he is one of the only survivors of Earth, I decided to ask him what his favorite memory of the planet was. I thought he might tell me about the end of World War IV or going to see *Spider-Man*, but instead he told me about the first date he went on with his wife, my great-grandmother Kathleen. They met in College, which is a place people used to go to after high school to drink alcohol. Some people drank so much there that they died.

My great-grandfather said that when he was in College, online dating hadn't been invented yet. Instead of matching with someone through a dating app and sending a series of nude photos to each other before eventually meeting up for sex, you would meet them in person before doing anything else. This meant that when my great-grandparents went out for the first time, they had no idea what each other looked like naked. At this point my mother, who was recording our interview, told my great-grandfather that he was being inappropriate because this was a project for school, and he apologized but said that the naked stuff was "crucial to the story" and that he was going to keep bringing it up whenever it was relevant.

My great-grandfather explained that not only had they not seen each other naked, he wasn't sure if my great-grandmother wanted that to happen. Sometimes, in those days, when someone agreed to go out on a date with you, they were still undecided about the naked thing and wanted to learn more personal information about you before making up their mind. Since this was before social media, the only way to get this personal information was by asking people questions to their face, like as if their actual living, breathing face was their social media profile. Sometimes this would get embarrassing. Like you might say, "What do your parents do?" And they would say, "My parents are dead." And then you would have to say something like, "I'm sorry. I didn't know that because I have no information about you. We are strangers." And sometimes the other person would forgive you, but sometimes they would not. Also, sometimes the person you'd asked out on a date would not even know it was a date because they assumed that you were gay, or they found you so unattractive that it had not even occurred to them that you might be pursuing them romantically—like that notion was so sick to them that it had truly not even crossed their mind. And sometimes they would convey this information to you in the middle of dinner—that they considered you a friend and nothing more—and to make the situation less humiliating, you would have to pretend that you felt the same way, and keep on smiling all night, even though you'd just learned that this person you hoped you might see naked was so repulsed by you that even though you had invited them to a Spanish restaurant, it had legitimately never entered their mind that you were hoping for intimacy, because that would be as insane as being asked out by, like, a dog or a potato.

The point, my great-grandfather said, is that he had no idea what my great-grandmother thought about him. He had no idea what she thought about *anything.* He had zero information about her, other than what she looked like wearing clothes, and also how it sounded when she laughed, which she had done a couple of times on their long, slow walk through campus, with the cool fall breeze whipping through the scattered leaves.

My great-grandfather said that all dates began with the same custom. The two people on the date would take turns verbally listing all the TV shows they liked. If they both liked the same show, they'd exchange memes from it. But here's the thing: GIFs did not exist yet. So instead of texting the other person a funny moment from the show, you would say out loud, "Do you remember the part when…," and then you would perform the meme yourself, using your face and body to imitate what an actor had said and done. Exchanging memes in person was much scarier than doing it by text, because when you text someone a meme and they don't respond, you can tell yourself that maybe they liked it but just didn't have time to text you back. But when you performed a meme with your body and the other person didn't like it, you would be able to tell, because instead of laughing they would just kind of sadly look away and say, "Yeah, I remember that part." And you would have to just keep on walking to the restaurant.

Luckily, though, my great-grandfather's meme performances went over well, or at least well enough to keep the conversation going. And while he still had no idea whether they would ever see each other naked, he knew it was at least technically still possible.

My great-grandfather had invited my great-grandmother to a Spanish restaurant because it was the only restaurant he knew that served wine to people under twenty-one. But when they arrived, it was too crowded to get a table. They needed to find some other place to eat, but neither of them had Internet access, so their only option was to physically search for food, by walking around and looking in random directions — like, truly the same process used by animals. Things grew tense. The sun had set, and my great-grandfather was fearful that they would not be able to find alcohol. But after a few stressful minutes, they followed the scent of fried food around a corner and found a Chinese place that served beer, and they were so proud of themselves that they spontaneously high-fived, and that was the first time that they touched.

My great-grandfather told me they stayed at the restaurant so long that by the end they were the only customers left. Because they were strangers, they asked each other very basic questions, like "Who are you? Where did you come from? What kind of a person are you?" They ended up having a lot of things in common, which was exciting, because that didn't usually happen on a first date. Often the other person would dislike things you liked, or love things that you hated, or things would seem to be going pretty well, and the person would seem really nice, but then out of the blue they would say, "What is your relationship with Jesus Christ?"

My great-grandfather said that the main thing he talked to my great-grandmother about was how nervous they both were about the future. I asked if he meant climate change, and he admitted that the imminent climate holocaust hadn't come up much, and instead they'd mostly talked about their careers. It turned out they both had the same dream: to write stories down onto pieces of paper. In fact, they were both already trying to do that. Every day, they would each type out stories on computers and then print them with ink onto pieces of white paper. Their goal was to get better at making these paper stories, in the hopes that someday, they might be able to persuade someone to reprint their paper stories onto multiple pieces of paper, and then sell those pieces of paper for pieces of money, which were also made of paper. At this point, my mother whispered to me that it was time for my great-grandfather to take a nap, and she gave him some medicine that made him sleep for about four hours. When he woke up, though, he was still insisting all this paper stuff was real, and that it was their actual shared ambition to write stories down on paper and then sell the paper for more paper. And my mother smiled and rubbed his hand and said she believed him, but while she was doing that she buzzed for the doctor, and he brought in this huge syringe that was almost like a gun, because it was made out of metal and it had this trigger on the bottom, and the doctor explained that he was going to shoot this thing into my great-grandfather's brain, to make him less confused. And my great-grandfather laughed weirdly and said that he had been joking about "all that paper stuff," and that really what he and his wife had talked about on their first date was climate change, because that's what any sane person from that era would have prioritized: being a climate warrior. And the doctor looked into my great-grandfather's eyes with his finger on the trigger, and said, "Are you sure?" And my great-grandfather swallowed and said, "Yep!" And so the doctor left, but on his way out, he told my mom that he would stay nearby in case my great-grandfather got confused again, in which case he would come back and give him that gunshot right in the middle of his brain.

My great-grandfather was quiet for a while, almost like he was afraid to keep going with his story. But I pressed him for more information, and he said the main thing he had wanted me to know before was not *what* he and my great-grandmother talked about; it was *how* they talked, because even though they were basically still strangers who had never even seen each other naked, they somehow believed in one another from the start.

My great-grandfather told me that all dates ended with the same custom. After the two people finished all the alcohol they'd been served, one person would ask the other to come over to their dorm room to watch

Arrested Development. Arrested Development was a non-*Spider-Man* show that you played by putting small, round discs into a machine. The reason it existed was to create a way for people on dates to gauge each other's interests in becoming naked without having to directly ask them. The way this worked was a little complicated, but my great-grandfather was able to explain all the steps. First you asked the other person if they had "seen *Arrested Development,*" and they would respond, "Some, but not all of it." This would be your prompt to ask them if they wanted to come to your dorm room to watch the episodes they'd missed. If they didn't want to see you naked, they would say that they had to "finish a paper," which was an expression that meant that they were not attracted to you. If they did agree to watch *Arrested Development,* it meant that they probably did want to see you naked. But here's where it gets complicated: sometimes it did not mean that. Sometimes it just meant that they wanted to watch *Arrested Development.*

That's why there was a third part of the custom. After walking back to your dorm room and putting one of the discs into the disc-playing machine, you would sit side by side on a small couch. Your eyes would be facing the screen, but your attention would be focused entirely on each other. As *Arrested Development* played, you would physically move closer to the other person, inch by inch, without making any sudden movements. The idea was that if you both moved incrementally toward each other, eventually your hands would touch. If the other person pulled their hand away or laughed and said, "Sorry!," that meant they had really, truly come to watch *Arrested Development*. But if they did not pull their hand away from yours, that meant it was time to start kissing, which is what my great-grandparents did, even though they had never exchanged even the most rudimentary of nudes, and at this point my mother told my great-grandfather to stop telling the story, and he had to admit that the next part was genuinely inappropriate.

My great-grandfather said that their marriage wasn't perfect. Sometimes they argued, and in the 2050s they both had full-fledged affairs with sex robots. But they ultimately forgave each other, because nobody's perfect, and also by the 2050s sex robots had become extremely advanced as well as incredibly persuasive— like if you refused to have sex with them, they would start making really high-level philosophical arguments about "why it wasn't wrong," using logic that was essentially bulletproof, while their boobs and dicks lit up and spun and stuff, and eventually it got to the point where the UN had to regulate the Sex Robot Industry, because they needed people to leave their apartments again so we could go back to being a society.

The point is, my great-grandparents rekindled their romance in the 2060s, and they even ended up renewing their vows while riding on the Escape Pod to New Earth, surrounded by their daughters and their grandchildren. And my great-grandfather asked my mom if she could remember the ceremony, and she said she was only four at the time, but she did vaguely recall how weird it was to see him on the spaceship when it was supposed to be just for women and children, and my great-grandfather said that they needed to bring one man to "help the women lift their bags into the overhead compartments," and I reminded him that earlier he'd said he'd been on the ship to row an oar, and there was a long pause, and then he said that he was tired and had to go to sleep. And he closed his eyes, but it didn't really look like he was sleeping, because every few seconds he would open his eyes to check if we were still there, and when he saw we were he would quickly close his eyes again.

And it was around this time that my great-grandmother rolled up in her wheelchair. And my great-grandfather stopped pretending to be asleep, and he sat up and smiled, and she smiled back, and then he lowered his voice and said, "Do you want to watch *Arrested Development?*" And my mom reminded my great-grandfather that *Arrested Development* had been lost, along with everything else on Earth, because of his generation's crimes against humanity. But my great-grandfather ignored her and motioned for his wife to wheel next to him. And he flipped through random channels, while their hands inched slowly toward each other.

And that's when I finally figured out what Earth was really like.

It was kind of like *Arrested Development.*

It was something people talked about, and praised, and maybe even tried to save, but the whole time, what everybody secretly, actually cared about was the person sitting next to them. That's where all of mankind's effort went, the sweat and the toil of billions, not to saving the world but to the frantic, desperate quest for love. And that's why Earth is gone, because it was nothing more than a conversation starter. It wasn't what we really, truly cared about. We never even really *lived* there. We lived in the presence of each other.

And when my mom read my first draft of this, she said that I shouldn't end it this way, because it's glib and defeatist and seems to absolve my great-grandfather of his political inaction, but it's not like anybody's going to read this stupid essay anyway, and even if they do it'll eventually be lost like everything else besides *Spider-Man,* so I'm just going to stop it right here, because I want to go out and the night's still young.

MARIO

It's-a me, Mario! I was-a working as a plumber in New York when I fell-a down a pipe and landed in the Mushroom Kingdom. Pretty soon, I was-a having all kinds of super-fun adventures, crushing Koopas, dodging hammers, and jumping through castle after castle. It's-a like my whole life was a game. I'd-a wake up each morning shouting, "Wahoo! Yiiiiippeee! Here we go!"

That feels like a really long time ago. I was-a born in 1984, which means, if you do-a the math, I'm-a forty years old.

I wasn't-a really thinking about it much until last summer. Just another birthday, right? Then it's-a like the reality of the thing just hit me. Like, "Mamma mia, I'm-a going to be middle-aged." It's-a like one of those fireballs that moves-a so slowly you forget it's even coming, until it's-a right in your face.

The thing that's so hard about turning forty is it

forces you to take-a stock of how you're doing. And to be honest, I'm-a not doing so great. These days, my life, it's-a fucked up. Like, there's just a lot of super-heavy shit that I'm-a dealing with right now. I guess the best way to explain it is-a to start from the beginning of last week, which is when shit really started to get-a, like, super fucked up.

Here we go...

★ ★ ★

So basically one day I wake up, and it's-a, like, I can't-a move my back. Like, at all. So I go to Dr. Mario (no relation), and he's-a, like, "Mario, when's-a the last time that you had a physical?" And I'm-a, like, "Can't you just look at my back like-a normal?" And he's-a, like, "No, because I'm-a starting to think there might-a be underlying problems." So I'm-a in this tiny room for hours, doing all kinds of tests that I've-a never done before, and finally Dr. Mario comes back holding some X-rays, and he says that between the jumping and the running and the smashing the bricks with my head, I've-a basically given myself arthritis. So I ask for a cortisone shot, and he's-a, like, "It's-a too soon since the last one." And I'm-a, like, "Come on, it's-a me, Mario." So he sighs and gives me one, right in the spine, and it's-a, like, literally the most painful experience of my life, but the sick thing is that I'm-a grateful. That's-a how fucked up my back is. I'm-a crying from agony and thanking him at the same time, because I know this shot, it's-a going to at least give me a few days of relief. And he says, "We need-a to schedule the surgery, Mario. The one we've been-a talking about. To fuse-a your spine. Recovery's-a going to be brutal, but the alternative is you could-a end up in a wheelchair. You could lose-a your ability to walk." And he gives me his card and writes down his cell phone number on it, and I'm-a thinking, "Mamma mia, it must be serious if he's-a giving me his private line." And I walk out of his office, and I'm-a staring at his card, and I'm-a just, like, "I can't face this." So I stick it under the shell of a passing turtle and give him a kick, and he slides across the bricks, just skidding off into oblivion.

So then I check-a my phone and there's-a, like, twenty missed calls from the Princess. And I just sigh, like, "Here we go." And I call her back and she's-a, like, "Who's calling?" And I'm-a, like, "It's-a me, Mario. Who the hell else would it be?" And she's-a, like, "I'm sorry. I guess I didn't know if you were going to call me back or not, because lately it's like you're not even a part of my life." And then she just starts-a going off on me for being out of touch all day, and when I tell her I was at the doctor she accuses me of lying to her, because at this point in our relationship there's-a, like, zero trust. And I'm about to hang up when she tells me she's-a been kidnapped by a Koopa.

And I know I'm-a not supposed to say this, but lately I've started to think she's been getting kidnapped by Koopas on purpose. The first few times it happened, I was-a, like, "Okay, that's a weird coincidence." But then it happened again, and again, and, like, literally thousands more times. And recently I said to her, "If you know that the Koopas are after the *Princess,* why do you walk around wearing a *crown?*" And she was, like, "Oh, so you're saying I was *asking for it? Because of the way that I was dressed?*" And I was, like, "You know what? If you want to get-a me canceled, go ahead!" Because, honestly, sometimes I fantasize about that shit since it would give me an excuse to stop. I wouldn't even do an apology, I'd-a just go off the grid, like Mega Man after that N-word thing, because at this point I'm-a so goddam tired, I'd just be, like, "Great, I'm out! Wahoo! Yiiiiippeee!" You know? Like, fuck it.

So anyway, she texts-a me the address of this castle she's trapped in, and it's-a, like, seven worlds away, with dozens of levels in between, plus mini games. And my back, it's-a already starting to tingle, which means the cortisone's-a wearing off. I have, at most, like, two days of mobility left before it's like I'm-a basically going to be paralyzed. And so I tell her, you know, "I'm-a sorry, but I can't save you this time. Even jacked up on stars and hauling ass, there's-a no way I can make it."

So she's-a, like, "Guess I'll call Devon."

And Devon, he's-a this DJ who's, like, twenty-two at most, and he's-a got that whole Machine Gun Kelly look, like, super tall and thin, with all the piercings and the neck tattoo. And I don't even think she's-a actually into him, but it doesn't matter. Because it's-a like she has this *power* over me, like, when she wants to hurt me, she can hurt-a me. Still, after all these years.

So I say, "Hey, come on, baby. Relax. It's-a me, Mario." And her voice gets soft, and she asks if I'm-a coming to save her or not. And I say, "Of course. Just wait on your floating block over the fire. I'll-a think of something."

So that night I'm-a frantically searching through these message boards about back pain, and I see there's this miracle device from Europe that's, like, an electronic belt that takes-a all the pressure off your spine. And I make some calls, and there's a guy downtown who's got one of these things, but it's-a going to cost $10,000. And I've-a got, like, five coins in my checking account.

And I know what you're-a thinking: "How does *Super Mario* go broke? You collected *entire rooms* of coins! What happened?" And the answer is-a simple: I trusted a close personal friend to manage-a my money. And I can't say too much about what happened, because the lawsuit is-a ongoing, but essentially, all those years I thought that I was riding Yoshi, it was the other way around. That dinosaur, he was-a fucking me from moment one. And I know I deserve-a some of the blame for not catching on, because by the end he had his own island, and safari, and there was even Yoshi's World. I mean, this guy got so rich he had his own *private world* named after him. But still, when you've-a known someone forever, and he's always just-a smiling and laughing and making little cooing sounds, you never think, "This guy's-a fucking me."

So anyway, the Princess is-a waiting for me, and I can't-a do shit until I get this spine belt, and that means there's-a only one move I can make. I've-a got no choice but to take the bus out to the suburbs and go see my brother.

So, look, here's-a the deal with Luigi. I'm-a glad he got sober, because, you know, he was-a going to die. And now he does four hours of yoga every day, and he and his husband, Kwame, they seem-a genuinely happy, and I'm-a happy for them. It's-a great. Wahoo, yippee. At the same time, I'm-a not going to pretend like it's a blast hanging out with them and all their dogs.

So I walk up to their fancy gate and ring the stupid

intercom and say, "It's-a me, Mario." And Kwame's, like, "Mario, what a pleasant surprise!" And this guy, he's-a nice, but he's-a more boring than World 1, Level 1, on Easy. He reads self-help business books for fun, and I've-a known him for three years and I still have no clue what he does. But I guess that he's-a loaded, because Luigi is essentially a professional sunbather now, and their driveway, it's-a, like, Tesla, Tesla, Tesla.

So they invite me in for lunch (but of course they're on a cleanse, so there's no pizza, no meatballs, no nothing). And I tell-a them my whole fucked-up situation—how the Princess is-a trapped, and I need to buy this spine belt, but I've-a got no money—and they say they're-a going to help me. And I'm-a super relieved. But instead of writing me a check, Kwame says, "Mario, are you familiar with the concept of a career pivot?" And I'm-a, like, "What?" And he tells me there's-a "no shame" in aging out of professional rescuing, and that it's-a not too late for me to transition into something less physically demanding. And he hands-a me this book called *What Color Is Your Parachute?* and says, "Hey, you know what might be fun? If we made you a new résumé right now!" And Luigi gives me a big thumbs-up, like I've-a just won a fucking extra life.

So Kwame takes out his laptop, and he's-a, like, "Okay, what would you say is your most marketable skill?" And I've-a got no choice but to play along, because I still have to hit them up for cash. So I'm-a, like, "I don't know, I guess fighting Koopas?" And Kwame's, like, "We *could* focus on your combat skills. But I think it might widen the net if we highlight your experience with plumbing." And Luigi rattles off the dates of my last plumbing job, and Kwame types them in, and then he's-a, like, "We need a strategy for how to explain the gap." And I'm-a, like, "What gap?" And he's-a, like, "You know, this multidecade period when you were out of the workforce." And I'm-a, like, "It's not like I was just sitting on a cloud all day. I was-a traveling from world to world, going on quests." And he's-a, like, "Right, but a plumbing executive won't necessarily interpret it that way." And he writes up this cover letter that's-a designed to turn "the negative into a positive":

Dear prospective employer,

I am writing to apply for the position of journeyman plumber at your company or business. Plumbing is a lifelong passion of mine. After beginning my career in New York City, I took a multiyear hiatus to the Mushroom Kingdom in order to improve my knowledge of pipes. Now I am ready to jump back in the game and pick up where I left off. I am confident that I am the right person to help you achieve success.

Sincerely, Mario Mario

And Luigi's, like, "Wow, that's-a perfect!" And I'm-a just reading it over and over again, like, really? All my adventures, the entirety of my adult life, it all boils down to a "hiatus"? And it feels like I've walked into a spike and gone from big to small, and all the mushrooms in the world can't make me big again.

And by this point the Princess is-a texting me nonstop, like, Where. The. Fuck. Are you. So I turn to Luigi and say, "Listen, I really appreciate all this great life advice, but today the main thing is, I need-a to borrow some money, so I can buy this spine belt and save the Princess from the Koopa." And there's-a this long silence, and eventually Kwame squeezes Luigi's hand, and Luigi takes a deep breath, and I'm-a just rolling my eyes, like, "Here we go." And Luigi takes off his hat and launches into this speech, which is obviously super rehearsed. And he's-a, like, "Mario, we want to help you, but we don't-a think we've-a been helping you in the right way. And that's-a why, for your sake and ours, we have-a decided to put up some financial boundaries." And that's-a when I kind of lose my cool and start running around shooting fireballs. And Luigi's, like, "Mario, don't-a do this." But I'm-a so angry now, it's-a like I'm just in battle mode. And Luigi runs at me, and I shoot him a look, like, "Let's-a go!" But even though I can usually take him, my back, it's-a so messed up that he manages to jump on my head, which makes me motionless. And these giant block letters appear over us, saying, "LUIGI WINS!" And he's, like, "I'm-a sorry, Mario." And I'm-a, like, "Fuck you."

And as I'm-a hobbling out of their dumb gate I pass-a this pile of Amazon packages. And I can tell it's all nice stuff, like P-Wings and POW blocks, and I remember how Amazon, they've-a got this policy where if something goes missing, they just reimburse you, no questions asked. And I'm-a thinking, you know, "Is it really a crime if nobody gets hurt?" So I grab a few packages, and as I'm-a walking to the bus stop I hear-a this voice in my head, saying, "You-a just robbed your own brother." But by this point it's-a like I'm just on autopilot, almost like I'm-a being controlled by someone else. (And obviously I know that sounds-a crazy, but that's-a how I'm feeling.)

So anyway, I pawn all this crap and call-a the guy who's got the spine belt. And he tells me I've-a got to pay him right now, over the phone. And I'm-a, like, "I've-a got to try it on first to make sure it works." And he just laughs, because I guess he can hear-a the desperation in my voice. So I say fine, and I Venmo-a him all of my money, and as soon as it goes through, he starts laughing even louder and talking about how much he loves garlic. And finally, I'm-a, like, "Wait a minute, who is this?" And he says, "It's-a me, Wario," and it turns out the whole thing was a scam. And it's-a basically the emotional low point of my entire life. I'm-a just crying on the sidewalk, you know? Like, Game Over.

And just when things-a can't get any worse, I see something skidding toward me. And I realize it's-a the turtle that I kicked outside Dr. Mario's the day before. It must've bounced off a pipe or a brick, and now, instead of sliding away from me, it's-a sliding right at me. And this thing's-a getting closer and closer, and I'm-a getting ready to jump over it, when all of a sudden time pauses. You know how that happens sometimes? Like, you'll be jumping or flying, and then, out of nowhere, everything in the world will freeze? Not seeing a lot of nods. Well, anyway, time pauses for me in this moment, and all these thoughts start-a swirling through my head.

And the first is this memory of the last quest I went on with Luigi. It was after he got out of rehab, but before he and Kwame started dating, although I think they were-a maybe hooking up by then. So anyway, we were-a swimming underwater, dodging jellyfish, and I notice he's-a kind of hanging back. So I'm-a, like, "Let's-a go!" And Luigi says, "What's-a the hurry?" And I'm-a, like, "What are you talking about? We're-a being timed, and the faster we go the more points we get." And he's-a, like, "Yeah, but what are the points for?" And at the time I just laughed, like, you know, *That's-a just Luigi being silly.*

But now, as I'm-a standing paused before this turtle, this thing he said comes rushing back to me. "What are the points for?" And I realize that he's-a kind of right. Because the truth is, the points, they don't-a really get you anything. You can't-a trade them in for prizes. Best-case scenario, your tally ends up on a high-score list, next to a word like "PEE" or "DIC," and even then, it's-a only a matter of time before the whole list randomly resets for no reason.

And then I start to think about my relationship with the Princess. Did I really want to be with her? Or was her love just another form of points? Another currency for me to amass to prove-a to myself that I had worth, and that, despite my immigrant background and high-pitched voice, I was-a still deserving of love? I'd-a been with the Princess for decades, but it's not like we'd-a ever actually connected. I barely even saw her, except for a few seconds after each rescue, and even then, it's-a not like we had deep conversations—we just stood next to each other, staring straight ahead, while some text scrolled anticlimactically over our heads, followed by Japanese names.

And as I'm-a having this realization, the world unpauses and the turtle continues sliding toward me. And instead of jumping over it, I decide to jump on top of it, which makes it motionless. And I reach under its orange shell, pull out Dr. Mario's card, and call-a his personal number and say, "It's-a me, Mario, and I need help."

And within thirty minutes I'm-a in his office signing consent forms for "anterior lumbar interbody fusion." And he's-a, like, "You're going to need someone to wash your body and help-a you use-a the bathroom, because for the first twelve weeks of recovery you're-a going to have zero mobility. Do you-a have a partner who can help you?" And by now the Princess has straight-up blocked my number, and I guess she did end up calling Devon, because she's-a posting all these pictures of him on social media, tagged, like, #realhero and #waybetterthanmario. So I'm-a, like, "Is there some kind of sponge on a stick that I can use to clean my ass?" And Dr. Mario, he's-a walking me through the different stick options when Luigi jumps through the window. And then Kwame comes in a second later, through the door (because he took-a the elevator).

And it turns out someone from Dr. Mario's office

called them up, because they were-a listed as my emergency contacts. And they tell Dr. Mario that they're-a going to help me recuperate, and they've already converted Luigi's solarium into my recovery room. And I'm-a feeling super guilty because there's no way they'd-a make this kind of offer if they knew that I'd-a stolen from them. And so I start to confess about the Amazon boxes, and Luigi says, "Mario, we know. We saw you pick them up and shout, 'Wahoo.' That's-a why we're here. It's-a obvious that you're in crisis. We knew how much physical pain you were-a in, but we had no idea you were suffering so much emotionally. And we're-a sorry about the résumé thing before. We both realized even as we were-a doing it that it was a terrible idea, and from now on we're-a going to try to be less prescriptive, and the main thing is, we love you, and we're-a with you for the long haul, no matter what it takes." And Kwame's, like, "We mean it. We want you to stay with us until you're back on your feet." And I'm-a looking up at these guys, and I don't-a know what to say, because I've-a been playing the game for forty years, but this is the first time that it's-a me who's being rescued.

★ ★ ★

And now it's-a the night before the surgery, so I'm-a fasting at Luigi and Kwame's (no pizza, no meatballs, no nothing). And it's-a gonna be a long time before I can jump or even walk. And the truth is, I'm-a never going to be "Super Mario" again. When I come out the other side of this, I'm-a going to just be plain regular Mario, a middle-aged guy with a slight limp.

But I've also been starting to think that maybe getting older's not all bad. Like, for example, this is a little embarrassing to admit, but my whole life I've-a struggled with body stuff, like things about my weight and how I look-a naked. It's-a why I wear the overalls even when it makes no sense for what I'm doing. But now that I'm-a in my forties I don't really think about my body anymore, and when I do it's-a to focus on the parts that I'm-a proud of, like my thick mustache and my big strong ass. And honestly, I can't tell you how liberating it is just to allow myself to feel-a sexy. Like, why can't a short fat guy be sexy? I feel-a sexy, and I'm not afraid to say I feel-a sexy. Like, hey, it's-a me, Mario, and I've got a big, strong, super-hairy ass and I'm-a sexy. Deal-a with it.

I've-a also noticed that the older I get, the less angry I am at my dad. I mean, it's-a weird he named me Mario when his last name was-a Mario, so that my name's-a Mario Mario. But he was a really serious alcoholic, like-a red wine for breakfast, so it's kind of a miracle he was able to say a name at all.

And as I was-a doing the math with Luigi, we realized that the day I'm-a scheduled to be discharged from the hospital happens to be my forty-first birthday. And I joked to him, "I should throw a party." But then once I'd-a said it I realized, "Wait a minute, that's exactly what I should-a do." And so we're-a really going to do it, a party in my recovery room, and I'm-a inviting everyone I know, including Dr. Mario and even the Princess and Devon, because why not? I mean, I don't expect her to come, but even if she did I think I'd be-a cool with it. When we got together we were both-a super young and everything that's happened was at least as much my fault as hers. And I don't think we'll ever be the kind of exes who go out for brunch or whatever, but when all's said and done I'm-a genuinely rooting for her happiness.

And as I was going through the hospital checklist with Luigi, like do we have-a slippers and *Yellowjackets* downloaded on the iPad, I started to feel a familiar sensation. And I realized that it was the way I used to feel between levels. Tomorrow at 5:30 a.m. (I know), Dr. Mario's going to hit me with that gas mask, and it'll be like going through a pipe from one world to another. And maybe I'll have to learn some new moves once I get there, but so what? I'm-a ready for the challenge. Like, for example, I really want to do a podcast, and this morning I pitched the idea to Luigi and Kwame, and they said they would help me, and we even came up with a name for it (*The Next Level with Mario*). And Luigi's going to read-a the commercials, and Kwame's-a going to be my first guest, because it turns out his job is actually pretty interesting. It's-a this thing involving currency prices, I think, or something about bonds. Anyway, we're-a going to be talking about it for two hours. And maybe we'll-a get a lot of listeners, but even if we don't it'll still be a learning experience.

These past forty years, I've-a had all kinds of ups and downs. I've-a won and lost, flown and fallen, jumped and been jumped on. I'm-a covered in scars and soon I'll have some more. But I'm-a not scared. I'm-a ready. Someday, I'll-a run out of continues, but in the meantime I've got plenty of lives left.

Here we go...

MILLENNIAL FABLE

Once upon a time, around 2010 or so, there lived a hard-working ant and a carefree grasshopper.

The grasshopper was hopping to his heart's content one sunny morning when the ant trudged by, bearing a large load.

"Why aren't you hopping?" chirped the grasshopper. "The summer is upon us, and the days are meant for dancing."

"I'm studying for the GREs," said the ant. "And I strongly suggest you do the same."

"Why would I waste this sunshine toiling?" scoffed the grasshopper. "I was thinking, we should try Four Loko before it gets banned." And then he shouted, "YOLO," because it was during that brief period of time when people actually did that.

The ant smiled smugly at the grasshopper. "It may be summer now," she cautioned. "But winter will soon be upon us. Failing to prepare is preparing to fail." And with that, she marched into a Starbucks to practice analogies.

The ant went on to graduate school, where she diligently gathered useful skills like coding and statistics. The grasshopper, meanwhile, got work as a barback and moved into a tiny nest in Bed-Stuy. By winter, he'd lost touch with the ant entirely, although for a few years he would get spam emails saying she'd invited him to join LinkedIn.

Then, in 2024, the grasshopper ran into the ant at a wedding. There were bags under her eyes and her antennae looked droopy. The grasshopper assumed she was tired from toiling, but it turned out she'd been unemployed for months. Meta had laid her off by email and all the skills she'd learned in school had been automated by artificial intelligence. Her 401(k) was drained, and she was close to defaulting on her student loans. In order to make her monthly payments, she'd had to move in with her dad and his girlfriend in New Jersey even though they had a really small apartment and there was zero privacy, like *none*. Like she hadn't seen them having sex or anything, but she'd definitely seen things that she wished she hadn't, like boundaries were blurring in the apartment about what was acceptable to wear in common areas.

"Got any coke?" she asked abruptly.

"Not on me," said the grasshopper.

"Fuck," said the ant. She drained her champagne flute, then his.

"I can't believe this is my life," she said, staring at her claws. "I did everything I thought I was supposed to do. While everyone was hopping, I was foraging and gathering and interning..." She shook her head slowly, a far-off look in her eyes. "This morning I saw my dad's balls. He was wearing a robe, but it was loose, and when he walked by the couch where I've been sleeping, bam. There they were. Like, can't miss them, eye level. Right in my face. His balls, man."

The grasshopper knew it was impolite to ask, but he couldn't help himself.

"How much do you owe?"

The ant hesitated. "Including undergrad?"

"Just tell me," said the grasshopper. "It's probably not as bad as you think."

The ant peeked at him through her claws.

"A hundred and sixty thousand dollars," she whispered.

"Holy *shit!*" the grasshopper said, his five eyes bulging. "That's crazy!"

"Who at this wedding do you think is most likely to have cocaine?" the ant said. "The cockroach?"

The grasshopper looked around. "Yeah," he said. "The cockroach."

And so the ant marched over to the cockroach, and while he didn't have cocaine, he did have pills.

★ ★ ★

The grasshopper wasn't sure what the moral of the story was. It wasn't "Work hard," obviously, but it wasn't quite "Be lazy" either. After all, it's not like the grasshopper's life had turned out great. Recently, he'd discovered a weird spot on his thorax, and because he had no health insurance, he just went online for a few minutes and self-diagnosed it as molting, and while that's probably what it was, what if it wasn't?

The truth was that all his friends were struggling. The cricket's band had broken up. The moth had been drawn in by crypto and lost everything. The caterpillar had become so insecure because of Instagram that she'd undergone a total metamorphosis, enlarging her wings to the point where she looked totally insane. The bee had moved into a super-remote hive in the country, and while he claimed it was a commune, it was obviously some kind of cult. He called the leader his queen, and himself a drone, and the whole thing just sounded like a Netflix documentary waiting to happen.

Their generation had been spawned with such high hopes and expectations. They were supposed to change the world. Where had they gone wrong?

The grasshopper was thinking about leaving the reception early when he saw the ant shuffling toward him. He could tell the cockroach's pills had kicked in. Her exoskeleton was slick with sweat, and her stinger was twitching in time with Bruno Mars.

"Let's dance," she slurred.

The grasshopper wasn't in the mood, but when he started to say no, she jammed a pill in his mouth. He tried to spit it out, but it dissolved on his tongue instantly.

"What was that?" said the grasshopper.

"We'll see, motherfucker!" said the ant, cackling.

The grasshopper was freaked out, but also intrigued. The ant was shaking her thorax at him now, beckoning him closer with her pincers. He'd had a thing for her since they were hatchlings, but it had never occurred to him to do anything about it. He told himself it was because he had no chance, but maybe this whole time he'd just been lazy?

Some older fleas were staring, but the grasshopper ignored them and followed the ant onto the dance floor, the music pulsing in his ears. Before long, he was spinning her around by the abdomen, his four wings fluttering out so wide they enveloped them completely, and all they could see was each other.

★ ★ ★

They woke up in the grasshopper's nest in Bed-Stuy, their twelve limbs twisted in a sweaty knot. They awkwardly untied themselves, unsure what to say. They knew they weren't right for each other. It wasn't their mismatched personalities and genitals so much as their dim prospects for the future. If they got together, they'd probably never be able to have offspring, or savings beyond what they could store in their digestive tracts. They weren't young anymore; they had to think about these things. Still, when the grasshopper suggested breakfast, the ant said yes.

They ate standing up in the grasshopper's messy kitchenette, then kissed tentatively, brushing each other gently with their feelers. The ant rested her head on the grasshopper's abdomen, and he stroked her antennae as the sun shone through his tiny window.

They had sex again, took a nap, ate some fruit, and watched a movie. Then they decided to go out, not to anyplace in particular, just sort of around. And as they inched across the vast sidewalk, where the bike racks loomed so tall they seemed to touch the sky, the moral of the story finally dawned on them: they were just bugs. They always had been. They had no control over the world. They had no control over their own lives. All they had was each other, and not for very long. They reached for each other's pincers. It was summer again, and this time they weren't about to waste it.

THE CITY SPEAKS

The young people never stop coming.

They show up in groups of twos and threes and cram themselves into my apartments, packing in so tight I can feel the walls begin to buckle. They toss their cigarette butts in my gutters. They leave their empty bottles on my stoops. They dance in my best fountain because they mistakenly believe it's the one from the opening of *Friends*. On Saturday nights they swarm my west side to poke my cobblestones with their stilettos, and on Sunday mornings they stink up my sidewalks with their brunch.

There's something else: they piss on me. Not once in a while. Every. Single. Night.

The first few times it happened I was so taken aback I thought, *Surely that must have been an accident.* Four hundred years in, I know the score. It's deliberate, it's frequent, and it's absolutely emotionally devastating.

A typical assault goes down like this. Some young people will be walking down one of my sidewalks late at night when one of them subtly hangs back from the group. Each time I delude myself into thinking things aren't going where I think they are. Like maybe they distanced themselves from their friends to take an important work call. But when they reach for the belt, I have to face reality: this is happening. And because I can't move besides the occasional very minor earthquake, there's nothing I can do but just lie there, motionless, and prepare to take my medicine.

When it starts, I try to go to a happier place in my mind. La Guardia's first hundred days in office. The completion of the High Line. But there's only so much mental jujitsu I can do. I mean, I'm getting pissed on. And they're staring down at me, just absolutely dead-eyed, and I'm looking up at them, like, *You don't have to do this. Please don't do this.* But they just keep pissing all over me.

What's really messed up is that some of them wear shirts saying they heart me. If that's the case, they sure have a funny way of showing it, pissing all over my face and in my mouth (the gutters are my mouth) each night. If that's what it means to heart someone, go heart Philadelphia, you psychopaths.

My point is, it's always been this way, from the flappers, to the teddy boys, to the hippies, the punks, and the hipsters. So how do I deal with the infestation? What do I do with all these vile young people? The same thing *they* do with the toxins in their bladder: I flush them right out of my system.

★ ★ ★

From the moment the young people arrive, I do everything I can to make them leave.

I dispatch my rats to their neighborhoods. I infest their apartments with my bedbugs. I send my choicest roaches up their drains.

If they try to bike my streets, I spew foul air from my manholes. If they try to walk my sidewalks, I hit them through my grates. When it's hot, I flex my grid to break their air conditioners. When it's cold, I clench my pipes so that their radiators all get crazy loud. I stain their best shoes with my sludge, shit on their haircuts with my pigeons, and give them gonorrhea from my Gowanus Canal.

Sometimes I ooze green liquid from my gutters, just to baffle them. Just to get them in the headspace of, like, "What the fuck even is this place?"

I raise their rents. It's not entirely up to me, but I've got a process and over time it tends to work.

But despite all this, they usually stick around. Sure, they might go home to their parents for a week over the holidays. But then they return, full of fresh confidence and urine. Because that's the thing about young people. If you want to make them leave for good, it's not enough to destroy their lives. You've got to destroy their dreams.

And so I take aim at their childish ambitions.

I shake their flyers from my poles, so their concerts go unseen.

I scatter their zines with my breezes and lose their fiction submissions in my post offices.

I rain on their low-budget film shoots, unless that would serve the story, in which case I *don't*.

I short out the sound during their open mics, so all their best bits go unheard.

I doom their modeling ambitions with my pizza.

If they're riding the L to an audition, I tighten my tracks to make them late, and if they try to text the casting agent, I suck all the Wi-Fi from my tunnels.

I conspire with Chicago to close their new show out of town. And if they somehow make it to a Broadway stage, I summon a plague and shut myself down just to spite them.

I make my days long and my nights lonely, and if my skyline must shine through their windows, I make it seem very far away.

Some hold out longer than others. But sooner or later, the U-Haul comes.

The young people lurch out of their walk-up, in their faded concert tees, carrying the same crap they showed up with, along with a new laptop to help with that new remote IT job, the one that started out as an ironic part-time gig and somehow morphed into their whole career.

They try to act chipper as they load the van, telling themselves the move is only temporary. A change of pace. A break from the grind. But I can feel the heaviness of their steps, the thud of their ragged sneakers on my asphalt, and I know the truth. I've broken them.

When the van is almost full, they have to make tough calls. Do they take the amplifier? The drafting board? And what about the books? Those requisite copies of Capote, Patti Smith, and Didion? To trash them is to admit something too bleak, so they lovingly pack them in a cardboard box, a redundant FREE sign carefully tacked to one side. They force a smile as they set it on my curb, but I can see through their delusions. When my garbage trucks arrive at 4 a.m., it's goodbye to all that, just more grist for my gears.

I see to it there's no traffic when they leave. For once, my streets are smooth and clear. When they pass through the Holland Tunnel, I nudge them along with a little extra breeze.

The U-Haul is silent except for the sound of their duffels jostling around in the back, scraping against that painting by a friend they once thought would be worth something someday.

As they cross my last bridge, they sneak one final glance over their shoulder. I always make sure to look extra beautiful when they do, angling my buildings to catch the sun just right. My skyline is a flashing smirk. My traffic is a blare of laughter. And as they drive across my border, I catch sight of their faces in their side-view mirrors, and I can see the creases by their eyes, the gray strands in their hair, the datedness of their Warby Parkers, and my ecstasy reaches new heights, because not only have I booted out my young, I've made them old.

★ ★ ★

The young people piss on me and I piss on them right back. And that's usually the end of things.

But not always.

Sometimes, a young person comes who's built a little different than the others. You can feel it in the way they piss on you, a certain steadiness and sense of purpose. I come at them with all the usual stuff: roaches, rats, the death of print media, and sooner or later it works. They fall out of fashion, out of favor, off the guest list, off the charts. But even though they're too old to piss on me themselves, they decide to stick around and piss on me in a whole new way: by helping the young.

They attend their shitty readings, openings, and work-shops.

They patronize their ill-conceived Kickstarter projects, even though they don't really want one of the personalized watercolors.

They mentor them, not in an official way, which would require some kind of set time commitment, but just, like, agreeing to read a script every once in a while, as long as it's not too long, like, probably fifty pages is the max.

They resist the impulse to steer them to their own past work, because it's no longer in style, and in hindsight pretty offensive.

They tell them stories from their youth, mostly to name-drop, but also because they think it might conceivably be useful.

They help them to achieve success, and when it starts to happen, they fight the urge to sabotage them even though it would be so easy and they could do it in a way where they probably wouldn't get caught.

They blurb their first book even though it made them jealous, and they don't hold it against them when their quote's not the one on the cover.

When they see the shit I'm doing to them, they say that they've been there and take them out for coffee or beer or some other diuretic. And bit by bit, they help to create a new generation of pissers, who collectively will piss on me with more power and volume than they could ever muster on their own, a generation that will someday inspire the next one to show up on my streets in groups of twos and threes, and pack themselves into my apartments, with new kinds of dreams I can't even conceive of, and the piss will continue to flow, a never-ending stream, spilling all over my face and chest (Queens is my chest) for all eternity.

And that's why, as much as I fear young people, I fear old people more: because once they stop trying to be young, that's when they can really do some damage.

That's when they can really leave a mark.

PARTICIPATION TROPHY

Dear Simon,

I'll never forget the day we met. You were dressed boldly, in orthopedic Velcros, yellow sweatpants, and an oversized *Far Side* T-shirt. You completed your ensemble with a mesh green pinny, which you debonairly or mistakenly wore as a necklace, your head thrust fetchingly through one of the armholes.

I was young then. Fresh out of my bulk-order box. I can see myself now as I must have looked to you on that warm spring day: a gleaming figurine of indeterminate age and gender, gazing alluringly from my plastic podium, my lithe limbs splayed in a vague athletic pose, perhaps running, perhaps swimming, or maybe even doing a non-sports thing, like debate or drama. In any case, my body glinted in the sun like gold.

Although you had signed up for only one event that field day—a relay race in which you ran in the wrong direction—you never questioned my presence in your life. When Ms. Musgrove handed me to you and said, "You tried your best," you pumped both fists in triumph. I'll never forget how you caressed me with your gentle, Yoo-hoo-scented hands. When you held me to your chest, I could feel your heart pounding, and though I knew it was partly because your body was so unused to exercise, I sensed that there was also something more powerful at play.

On the bus ride back from Randall's Island, you held me on your lap, completely smitten. You carefully sounded out my engraving—"If you had fun, you won"—and while your reaction was muted at first, you eventually figured out that the sentence rhymed, which thrilled you to your core. I remember how you laughed hysterically, tears streaming down your face, as you repeated the rhyme to yourself, over and over again, and then to the other children on the bus, to make sure they also knew about the rhyme.

When you got home, you whisked me to your room and put me in a place of honor, next to your *Mad* magazines on the highest bookshelf you could reach.

And then your brother got home from bar mitzvah lessons. And in between bites of his intimidatingly sour candy, he told you that our love was a lie.

"It's not a real trophy," he said. "They give it to everyone, whether they're good at sports or not. They even give it to kids who are—" And then he said a word that isn't said anymore but that you both used to say constantly.

He told you I was "cheap" and "made in China" and not, as you'd assumed, "made out of real gold."

You defended me the best you could, but when he left, I could tell something had changed between us. Your brother had taken me off your shelf for demonstration pur- poses. Now that he was gone, you did not put me back.

Years passed. And with the exception of one afternoon during puberty when you became very curious about my butt, you moved on.

I was banished to a crate inside your closet. Meanwhile, you went off to prep school, in search of more glamorous conquests. First came those waifish science fair certificates, dressed up in their showy, gilded borders. Then that buxom chess cup, with its obscenely leering mouth. By the time you graduated high school, there were Latin plaques and honor pins and a slew of whorish Model UN gavels, stacked up on the shelf I once called home.

If you spoke of me at all, it was with ridicule.

"Remember participation trophies?" you'd scoff. "Those were so—" And then you would say that word that people don't say anymore but that you continued to say for longer than most people did.

You went off to college, where your taste grew even more refined. You were after high-class trophies now, medals made out of real metal, or whose names were at least searchable online. After graduation, you had your diploma framed and set out lustfully into the world.

Your twenties were a blur of striving, writing for TV. And while *The Daily Show* pretty much won every award every single year, you managed to pick up a couple. But there were always bigger trophies to win, so you kept on pushing, even after your children were born. And sometimes they would run into your office, in their Velcro shoes and oversized T-shirts, and try to play with your existing trophies by making them kiss each other. And as you ushered your kids out of your office, you wondered if participation trophies still existed. You doubted it, but you couldn't be completely sure, because you didn't attend many of their athletic events. The school was kind of far away, and you were busy.

And then one day, you heard your children running down the hall, and you sighed, dreading the inevitable interruption. But instead of barging into your office like always, they slipped by silently, and you felt a sharp pang in your chest, like someone discovering, in the middle of a relay race, that they'd been running in the wrong direction.

And you thought about the picture books you'd flipped through two pages at a time,

the half-assed baths and phoned-in Hokey
Pokeys, the fake trips to the bathroom at
that birthday party, writing notes to yourself
in a dank Chuck E. Cheese stall. And it
wasn't just the kids; it was everything: your
offensively generic anniversary cards, your
neglected text chain with your college friends,
the disturbingly corporate guest list for your
birthday party, the sand in your laptop and
the unpacked snorkel, the decades marked by
milestones rather than memories. And it
occurred to you that maybe all this time,
instead of ignoring life, or scavenging it for
material, you should have...what's the word
I'm looking for?

Oh yeah.

Participated.

Maybe what we had was real. Maybe it's
the rest of your life that's been—I won't say
the word, but you know the one I mean.

And now you're not young anymore. Your
surface is peeling, your figure is drooping.
Unlike me, you're biodegradable.

But here's the crazy thing: even though
you've spurned me, mocked me, and, on that

afternoon I mentioned during puberty, confused the hell out of me, I haven't given up
on you.

I know we won't be reunited. You're in Los
Angeles and I'm in a landfill, buried under
four hundred tons of WOW potato chips.
You could search a million years and never
find me. But maybe you can find that part of
yourself you left behind on Randall's Island,
the part that was present and grounded and
found joy in a rhyme that *barely worked.*

Through your office door, you can hear
the muffled tap of little feet. You're behind,
but the race isn't over. For God's sake, turn
around. Pass the baton. Go out there and
prove yourself worthy of my love.

II

TIME

The days were getting shorter. Twenty-three hours one month, twenty-two the next. Scientists couldn't explain it. The earth kept spinning faster and faster, like an out-of-whack carnival attraction, and there was nothing anyone could do to stop it.

We tried to live like everything was normal. The government switched us to a "relative clock," with each hour corresponding to one twenty-fourth of the day. It was comforting at first. *The Tonight Show* still began at "eleven thirty," and technically it still lasted "sixty minutes." But man, that show got weird. Jimmy Fallon barely had time to tell one joke before the first guest sprinted out from the wings, the Roots playing faster than a polka band. In high definition, you could see everyone sweating.

There were physical side effects that made no sense at all. We all gained weight, our backs started aching, and our hair fell out in clumps. I pretended not to notice when Jenny got wrinkles, suddenly and permanently, over the course of a long weekend, and she looked the other way the night seven hairs wormed their way out of my earlobes. Our libidos went down. We both looked saggy, droopy, and worn out. Whenever we posed for a picture, it took us a few tries to get one we both liked.

I was trying to make it as a novelist, but it was getting harder to find the time to write. A few errands could take up your whole day. A trip to Trader Joe's, a phone call with Time Warner. By the time you sat down to start a chapter, it was time to start thinking about dinner.

The bills were arriving faster and faster, so I took a job at the law firm where I temped. The commute felt longer than the workday. By the time I got into the office and answered a few emails, my boss was already splitting for the golf course, and why stay after that?

Days were down to under ten hours when I proposed to Jenny. We had a small ceremony, but by the time we finished writing all the thank-yous, we'd been married seven months. Jenny went off birth control and got pregnant instantly. Her belly swelled so quickly we could see it expanding, like a slowly inflating balloon.

First step, first word, first birthday. We said we'd write it all down in a journal, but we never got around to it. Mia was out of the crib before we'd finished build-ing it. And then one morning, when she was one or two or three, "Shake It Off" by Taylor Swift popped up on some playlist, and even though Jenny and I were a bit sick of that song, it was Mia's first time hearing it, and she started to do this dance where she was running in place as fast as she could while spinning her arms around and screaming, and when the rap break started, she turned to us with an almost angry expression, like, *Why haven't you played this for me before?* And then when that part ended, and there's that big "Whoa-oh-oh" thing, to transition back to the chorus, she collapsed on the carpet and let out a sound like *"Gaaaaaaahhhh."* And it was only when the song ended that we realized the ice cubes in our drinks were still solid. Time, for three and a half minutes, had slowed to its natural pace.

We called up the Pentagon and they dispatched their scientists to our apartment. They covered our bodies in electrodes and subjected us to months of testing. Even-tually, they managed to confirm our observations. For reasons no one could explain, the physical act of Jenny and me watching our daughter listen to a hit song for the first time managed to restore temporal balance to the universe.

There were some caveats. Jenny and I both had to be paying attention to Mia while it happened, with our phones out of sight and no side talk. We couldn't be hungover or mad at each other about something. And most crucially, the song had to be an absolute banger, something on the level of "Like a Prayer" by Madonna or "I Want You Back" by the Jackson 5. A song that was merely good, like "Dirrty" by Christina Aguilera, or cool, like something by the Strokes or whatever, wouldn't cut it. It had to be something undeniable, something that would make Mia just completely lose her shit.

Congress commissioned a task force to assemble a playlist of viable songs. There were fewer than we expected, thirty-one in total, plus a few maybes, like "California Gurls" by Katy Perry and the song from *Flashdance*. Scientists instructed us to play Mia one song per week, on Saturday mornings, after she ate pancakes. The syrup in her system would help ensure that her dancing was sufficiently crazy to have the intended effect.

The UN made sure each country knew when we were going to play one of the bangers, so people could take advantage of each temporal slowdown. With the exception of "Bohemian Rhapsody," they didn't provide us with a lot of time, but it was enough to restore some small semblance of normalcy to Earth. For a few minutes, people could stop rushing. Some used the intervals to write crucial work emails. Others had overdue conversations with their loved ones, to beg forgiveness, offer it, or say goodbye. A lot of people just rocked out to whichever hit we were playing, tapping their feet, or singing along if they knew the words.

It was left to our discretion which order to play Mia the songs in. We decided to go alphabetically, starting with ABBA.

We're already up to Jay-Z.

It's scary each time a song ends. The earth speeds up so fast, we lose our footing, and by the time we lurch up off the ground, it's the middle of the night. But there's also grounds for optimism. Many of the scientists stationed in our living room believe there might be other Mia-related ways to slow down time. There are experiments in progress involving sprinklers, and an interesting general hypothesis about vacations. A contingent from Stanford is doing a study on board games, and their MIT rivals are writing a monograph on tag. A bearded crank from Caltech has declared himself a "Disneyland absolutist," and even though his tone's a bit aggressive, his theory doesn't strike us as illogical. We're willing to try anything and everything, a rigorous trial and error approach. There's still lots of data to collect. The truth is, we've barely gotten started.

PUNISHMENT

And so it came to pass that the Lord created two humans in His image, called Adam and Eve. And He put them in the Garden of Eden and provided them with everything that they could want. And all He asked in return was that they not eat from the Tree of Knowledge. But lo, it came to pass that they did eat from this tree. And when the Lord saw that they had disobeyed Him, He was filled with wrath. And so He said to Eve, "Because you have done this, I will make your labor pains severe, and you will suffer greatly during childbirth." And to Adam He said, "From this day forth, you will work by the sweat of your brow in the fields, and indeed you shall die there, for you are made of dust, and to dust you shall return." And He banished Adam and Eve from the Garden and brought forth His Angel to guard it with a flaming, whirring sword for all eternity. And when

Adam and Eve were out of earshot, the Lord turned to His Angel and said, "Was that too harsh?"

And the Angel stared back at Him and said, "Uh, *yeah*, probably. They ate one piece of fruit."

And the Lord groaned and said, "Why didn't you stop me?"

And the Angel said, "We're supposed to be a united front. If we contradict each other, it'll just make them confused." And she shook her head and said, "What was with that 'dust' thing?"

And the Lord sighed and said, "I don't know. I knew it was crazy even while I was saying it, but I couldn't stop myself. It was just, like, out of nowhere I heard my dad's voice coming out of my mouth."

And the Angel said, "Well, I guess we should go talk to them."

And the Lord said, "What do you mean?"

And the Angel said, "You know, to tell them we changed our mind about the punishment."

And the Lord said, "I think we've got to stick to it."

And the Angel said, "Why? You just said yourself that it was overkill."

And the Lord said, "Yeah, but if we don't follow through, they'll never take anything we say seriously ever again!" And He handed her the sword and set it on fire and told her to start whirring it.

And the Angel said, "I really don't think we're going about this the right way."

And the Lord said, "Just let me handle the discipline, okay? I know what I'm doing."

★ ★ ★

And so the Lord stuck to the banishment thing. But despite the harsh punishment, the humans continued to sin. And one day the Angel showed the Lord a note from school, and He was, like, "Fuck, this is some major shit."

And the Angel said, "Yeah, they're starting to have real behavioral problems. We should talk to a psychologist and get some advice on what to do."

And the Lord said, "There's only one thing we *can* do: bring the hammer down."

And the Angel said, "What? Why?"

And the Lord said, "Because we set a precedent with that fucking fruit thing! If we don't punish them *at least* that much for all this new stuff, they're going to think that sodomy and murder aren't as bad as, like, sharing one small bite of an apple."

And the Angel said, "I've actually been reading a lot about this lately, and most experts agree that punishments are counterproductive."

And the Lord said, "So, what, we're just supposed to let them do whatever they want and become drug addicts?"

And the Angel rolled her eyes and said, "I'm obviously not saying that I want them to become drug addicts." And then she added, softly, "This is why we should've signed up for that parenting class."

And the Lord said, "That class was bullshit!"

And the Angel said, "How would you know? You refused to even read the description on the website."

And the Lord said, "It was held in the basement of a *toy store*! It was obviously just a scam to sell us toys!"

And that was how the conversation ended, without any resolution about the whole discipline thing.

And so the Lord punished the humans more and more, with floods and plagues and entire centuries without any television. And He kept giving them new rules, some of which made sense, but some of which were arbitrary, like "Don't mix milk and meat," which was something He'd just blurted out one morning when He was half asleep but now felt obliged to stick to, because if He didn't, He'd lose all credibility forever. And it got to the point where He could barely even keep track of the rules that He had made, or what the penalties were for breaking them. And so the humans were punished inconsistently, in ways that had more to do with His frustration level than with any kind of actual philosophy or game plan. Like, sometimes the humans would have punishments heaped upon them for basically no reason, and sometimes they'd do something truly messed up and get no punishment at all, or even be rewarded with political office.

And the Angel would say, "What happened to being consistent?"

And the Lord would tell her some bullshit about how it was a Test, but really it was just that He was completely overwhelmed and exhausted and also privately kind of stressed out about money.

And so it came to pass that there was basically, like, zero continuity. And so one day, in desperation, the Lord suggested that they pick the ten main rules and engrave them on a pair of large stone tablets.

And the Angel said, "A, they're never going to follow that, and B, it's completely unenforceable. Like, the only way to police it would be to watch them around the clock, which would be more of a punishment for us than it would be for them."

And the Lord finally broke down and admitted that the Angel was right, and that the tablet thing was crazy, and that He'd only suggested it because He was so beat down and broken and stressed out about money that He didn't know what the fuck to do anymore, about anything.

And the Angel said, "What is going on with you? You can tell me."

And the Lord took a deep breath and confessed His secret fear: "I feel like the humans are becoming bad people, and it's all because of me."

And the Angel took His hand and said, "That isn't true."

And the Lord looked hopeful and said, "So you think the humans are turning out all right?"

And the Angel said, "No. They obviously have some real issues. But I don't think it's all because of you."

And the Lord said, "Everything's all because of me. I'm omnipotent."

And the Angel said, "I think maybe, when it comes to creating humans, no one is. Sure, you can guide them a little here and there, and, like, obviously it's possible to really fuck them up—like, that's been proven with those Romanian-orphanage studies. But in general, you can't control what kind of people they become. No matter what you do, they kind of just end up turning into . . . themselves."

And as her point was sinking in, the Lord looked down and saw that the humans had started a new war. And He was going to do what He normally did (punish everyone involved, whether they'd started it or not), but instead He turned to the Angel and said, "Maybe we should go out tonight?"

And the Angel said, "What about the flaming sword?"

Because she'd been whirring it around this whole entire time.

And the Lord was, like, "I'm sorry I made you do that. You can put it down. That was just me being nuts."

And so they dressed up and went out for the first time in eternity. And they ordered drinks and appetizers and the whole thing. And they talked about fun subjects that they couldn't discuss when the humans were around, like whether or not Heaven was real, and how the secret numerical code in the Bible really worked. And they had so much fun that it felt like they were back In the Beginning, before they had humans, or even any animals, and it was just the two of them floating around among the sun and moon and stars.

And it came to pass that spending some time away from the humans made them feel better about having had them. And the Lord quoted some of the cute things He'd overheard them saying lately, like "I have a plan for my future" and "Here is the forecast for tomorrow's weather." And the Angel showed the Lord photos of some of the cute crap they'd built recently, like forts and towers and cities, and even though the Lord knew that it was going to be a pain in the ass to clean it all up, and that the humans would probably cry when He knocked it all down, He also had to admit it was adorable.

And they stayed out so late that they lost track of

time, and their babysitter, Satan, texted them saying the next hour would be $40, because after 10 p.m. counted as overtime.

And the Lord said, "Maybe we should find a different sitter."

And the Angel said, "There's no one else. I've checked."

And the Lord told her how grateful He was that they were doing this crazy thing together, because even though it was an absolute shit show most of the time, there was no one in the universe He'd rather create humans with.

And the Angel smiled and said, "Do you ever think about creating more?"

And the Lord said, "No fucking way. I mean, where would we even put them?"

And the Angel shrugged and said, "We could add another continent, or, if that's too expensive, put up drywall."

And the Lord laughed and said, "You're insane! If we add more humans, we'll never have a handle on things."

And the Angel said, "Yeah, but maybe *they* will."

And the Lord was taken aback, because He'd never considered that possibility, that someday the humans would know things He didn't, fix problems He couldn't, make new things He wouldn't. He'd been trying and trying to mold them in His image, but maybe they never would be. Maybe, instead, they'd be better.

RIDING THE RAILS

It had been Josh's idea to take the train. But two hours in, it was obvious Meghan had been right. They should have flown, whatever the cost—anything to shorten the ordeal of traveling with the twins. All comic books had been rejected. The UNO cards lay scattered on the floor. The only game the boys would play was one of their own invention, in which they took turns punching each other in the chest. They were obviously hungry but had rebuffed every snack, from the naively packed bag of baby carrots to the chocolate Zbars that normally served as a last resort. They were beginning to develop territorial feelings toward their armrest—a situation that could end only in violence—when Josh tapped Meghan on the shoulder.

"Sorry," he said, "I've got to use the bathroom."

"Again?" Meghan asked. She was crouched in the aisle, groping around for the water bottles the boys had lost before they'd even left Penn Station.

"Yeah, sorry," Josh said. "Something I ate."

Meghan gave his calf a sympathetic squeeze as he slipped past her and bounded down the aisle, the din of the children fading blissfully away with every step. Josh didn't actually need to use the bathroom, nor had he the three previous times, but he was desperate for a break. And whatever guilt he felt for lying melted away when he found himself in an empty gangway, standing alone between two cars, with the cool wind rushing through his hair. He closed his eyes, reveling in the taste of freedom.

"Nice con you're running," said a low, gruff voice. Josh looked down, startled to discover he wasn't alone. Huddled by his feet was a short, grizzled man in battered overalls and a porkpie hat. He held a bindle over his shoulder, and a corncob pipe between his lips.

"What con?" Josh asked.

"The ol' bathroom act," said the man, admiringly. "You hoodwinked the missus good. Now you're free 'n' easy, and she's none the wiser!" He leapt spryly to his feet and thrust out a grimy hand. "Name's Boxcar Benjo," he said. "I've been riding the rails since I was no bigger 'n my bindle, and it's rare to meet a jack as slick as you."

Josh smiled bashfully as he shook Benjo's hand. "I guess it was a little clever," he allowed. "I mean, she can't get mad at me for going to the bathroom."

"No sirree," said Benjo. "And now you can check your email, watch TikTok videos—hell, just stare off into space, like you're dead."

"Yeah," Josh said. "This is the life. It's been five minutes, though. I should probably get back."

Benjo flashed a toothy grin. "That's one way to play it," he said. "Or you could feed her some more flimflam."

"What do you mean?"

Benjo glanced over his shoulder to make sure no one was listening, then continued in a whisper.

"You could tell her there was a *line* for the bathroom."

Josh's eyes lit up with excitement.

"She'd buy that for sure!" he said. "I mean, there's lines for bathrooms all the time!"

"Bingo," said Benjo, pointing at his bulbous nose. "And even if she doesn't eat the biscuit, how's she gonna prove you lied? She wasn't over by the bathroom! She was with the kids! What's she gonna do, go interview everybody on the train? March up and down the aisle with a little spreadsheet, asking everybody when they went to the bathroom and for how long?" He laughed and slapped his knee.

"You're right," Josh said. "That's unlikely."

"Here, take a wallop."

Benjo handed Josh a flask. Josh hesitated briefly, then took a sloppy pull, the moonshine dribbling down the collar of his golf shirt. "Maybe I can get away with ten minutes," he said, as the liquor warmed his chest.

"Why stop there?" Benjo said. "Might as well run the ol' milk con while you're at it."

Josh leaned in with interest. "What's the milk con?"

Benjo rubbed his hands together. "Here's how you hack it. First you go to the dining car and buy yourself two cartons of milk. Now sure, that'll set you back a couple clams. But it'll be worth it. Because when you get back to the seats, and she says, 'Where were you? You were gone for half an hour,' you can say, real dramatic-like, 'Somebody had to get the kids milk.' You put it all on her, see? Like, you're the good parent, and she's the bad parent, because you remembered the kids needed milk and she wasn't even thinking about milk!" He laughed and slapped his knee again.

"Huh," Josh said. "Yeah, I don't know about that one."

"What's wrong with it?"

"I don't know," Josh said. "I just feel like that would lead to conflict."

"Not if you know your onions," Benjo said. He hooked his thumbs around his overall straps and leaned in. "Here's how you groove it. Later today, when she says she wants to talk to you about that weird passive-aggressive comment you made earlier on the train, about the milk, you say, 'Sure, let's talk about it.' But then when she asks you why you had a tone before, you say you *didn't* have a tone, and that she just *imagined* it, because she's crazy. And, you know, you just try to make her feel like she's crazy."

"Huh."

"What's wrong now?" Benjo asked, a bit defensively.

"I just think I'd feel a bit guilty gaslighting her like that," Josh said. "Especially given that it was my dumb idea to take the train."

Benjo's eyes twinkled. "Who's to say it was?" He jabbed Josh's chest with his finger. "Here's how you grease it. You tell her the train was *her* idea. And when she denies it, you say she's misremembering things because she's crazy. And, you know, again, you just keep saying over and over again that she's crazy."

"I'm not doing that," Josh said.

"Never said you should!" Benjo said, holding his palms up. "You're putting words in my mouth, like you always do when you have PMS."

Josh sighed. "I'm starting to think it was a bad idea to get advice from you."

"Yeah, probably," Benjo admitted. "I mean, my life is pretty horrible. I've never had a healthy romantic relationship."

"Because you're so passive-aggressive?"

"That, and the fact that I constantly masturbate in

front of strangers. That's my whole thing. I stay here all day between these cars, and when people walk by, I do it."

"You didn't do it with me, though."

"I'm not attracted to you."

"Oh."

The men were silent for a beat, swaying back and forth in the dark.

Josh checked his phone. "Look, this has been a really fun eight minutes," he said. "But I just don't think I can live this lifestyle anymore. Family's a lot of work, and sometimes it makes you feel like running away. But if you try to take shortcuts, and shirk your responsibilities, you just end up..."

"Alone?" Benjo ventured.

Josh pointed at his nose. "Bingo."

"Ooh, someone's coming," Benjo said. He hopped into the shadows and giddily undid his overall flaps. "Sounds like a group!"

Josh gave his friend a tender wave goodbye and walked off in the opposite direction.

★ ★ ★

Meghan was still crouched in the aisle when Josh got back to the seats.

"Sorry I was gone so long," he said.

"Big line?" she asked.

Josh took a deep breath. "No."

Meghan stood up and sniffed his collar with confusion. "Have you been drinking?"

"Yes," Josh admitted.

"Are you sure that's a good idea with your stomach?"

"I'm not actually sick," Josh confessed. "I've just been pretending to be, so I could escape parenting."

"Oh," Meghan said softly. She sat down and looked out the window, a blank expression on her face.

"I'm really sorry," Josh said. "It was wrong. I screwed up."

Meghan said nothing.

Josh sat beside her and squeezed her hand. "Honey?" he asked. "Are we going to be okay? Can you forgive me?"

"I'm stoned," she said.

"What? Really?"

"Yeah. I took an edible two hours ago, and it was a kind I've never tried before, and I think it was too many milligrams and that's why I can't find the water bottles."

Josh watched as the boys kicked the seats in front of them while chanting the word "butt."

"I've got a plan," he said. "A way to keep them quiet for the rest of the trip."

Meghan turned toward him. "Really? How?"

Josh rubbed his hands together. "Here's how we groove

it. We give the boys our phones, and then just let them do whatever on our phones."

"Why stop there?" Meghan said, a gleam in her eye. "We could download some video games and just let them play video games."

"Yeah, what are they gonna do?" Josh said with a sly grin. "Hit each other while fully engrossed in addictive video games? I'd like to see that!"

Meghan slapped her knee and laughed. "Yeah!"

They downloaded *Crazy Gears* onto their phones and handed them over to the boys, who both instantaneously fell silent. Then Josh lifted the armrest so Meghan could lie on his shoulder.

"This is the life," he said.

"I wouldn't go that far," Meghan said, closing her eyes. "But I sure love you."

Josh kissed her on the forehead. "I love you, too," he said.

TOOTH FAIRY

ToothCo is the big refinery in Fairy Land. We harvest the teeth and they melt them down for industrial applications—flame retardant, fertilizer, that sort of crap. Our CEO made $60 million last year, but none of that trickles down to us fairies. We're considered "independent contractors," which is a fancy way of saying they can fuck us any way they want. We're all assigned night shifts—no exceptions. And even though we're in bio-hazard collection, we're expected to work without protective gear. We're sick all the time. Pink eye, rotavirus, foot-and-mouth. And that's nothing compared to the injuries. We're only two inches tall and (unlike some) we don't have a fancy sled. We've got to duck and weave through miles of hail, fight our way through kites and mini drones. Inside the homes it's even worse: dogs, cats, booby traps set by imaginative children. One time I had to chew my own wing off to escape from a

Vornado. When I got back to the factory, I requested medical treatment, and these two huge men I'd never seen before took me straight into a back room and made me sign a form that said that I would never sue, even if my "injuries proved permanent." We tried to unionize once. All we wanted was extra pay for molars. They threatened to replace us all with sprites. We were back on the lines in forty minutes. We don't get any benefits, not even dental, which feels personal. Our wands are defective. Our fairy dust is toxic. They make us buy our own tutus from the company store, and if you've been doing this as long as I have, you know to order yours a size up, so you can slip in some Depends. (That's the Tooth Fairy version of a "break room.") It's like being an animal; every day, you're just trying to survive.

Each fairy is assigned one Tooth Producing Unit (aka child) at a time. That doesn't sound like much, but you've got to be on call 24-7, since kids can spit one out at any moment. Sometimes you get lucky, and the tooth is immediately accessible (in a pile of sand under some monkey bars, say, or lodged inside a water park filtration system). Usually, though, a parent holds on to the tooth so they can enact some kind of BS ritual with their child.

I have no idea where all these rituals come from. All I know is that they make a hard job even harder. First,

I've gotta wait for the parent to put the tooth under their kid's pillow, then the kid's got to fall asleep, then finally, by eight or nine if I'm lucky, the parent tiptoes in, slips the kid some cash, and grabs the payload. If they toss it in the trash, I'm golden. I just wait until their back is turned, dive inside, and haul that sucker to the smelter. If they stick it in a drawer, it's not so bad. I'll wait a day or two for them to forget about it, then come back and swipe it then.

Once in a while, though, you get a rotten deal.

Once in a while, you end up with parents like Todd and Allie Jensen.

From the moment I see these two, in their matching his-and-hers pajamas, I know I'm in for it. They've baked a "first tooth cake" in honor of their daughter's grand achievement, and they're passing out pots and pans so they can do a "tooth parade." It's ten minutes of banging and singing, then another ten of them centering the tooth under the pillow. When the kid finally conks out, they stand in her doorway for a solid hour, watching her snore, squeezing each other's hands, exchanging wistful looks. My patience is already thin when they decide to write the kid "a letter from the Tooth Fairy" in glitter pen.

Dear Maggie,

I just heard the "fang"-tastic news that you've
lost your first tooth. Talk about a "crown"-
ing achievement!
    I also want to say how "enamel"-ored I am
by your good brushing habits. Dr. Wu would
be proud, and that's the "tooth"! ("Truth.")
                              Love, Tooth Fairy

The letter offends me on a number of levels, but I'm
just thinking, you know: *At least this shit is almost over.*
No such luck. After Todd tiptoes in and grabs the tooth,
he hands it to Allie, who polishes it with some kind of
professional-grade cleaning gel. Then he takes out this
fucking thing from Etsy—a wooden heart-shaped plaque
with twenty holes in it—and with the precision of two
bomb defusers, they place the tooth inside the hole
marked "#1," and as they're screwing a Plexiglas lid
over the top, I realize: I'm fucked.

★ ★ ★

If you don't hit your quota, you're labeled an "under-
performing fairy" and put on an "improvement plan."
What that means, essentially, is they begin to torture
you. Sleep deprivation, water restriction. At some point

a tribunal declared that they have to give us gumdrops, so we don't literally starve, but it's basically hell until we start producing.

I start working overtime at the Jensen house, scouting around, looking for any kind of angle. They live in one of those cheesy new construction deals, a gray-brick, white-trim cube at the end of a cul-de-sac. There's a blindingly white Toyota Sienna in the garage and a pair of Target garden gnomes guarding the featureless front lawn. Inside, Todd types energetically in his beige home office, the official headquarters of Todd Jensen Web Design. Allie helps him mail out doodads to potential clients: cheap pens and desk calendars, emblazoned with his corny logo. They lovingly swaddle the swag in Bubble Wrap while gossiping about their neighbor Karl, whose occasional cigarette smoking manages to scandalize them both. Hopper, the Labradoodle, yaps through the house with impunity, while Maggie dances endlessly to *Moana*, twirling in place in the living room, beneath a faux wood "Live, Laugh, Love" clock. Their routine never changes and, unfortunately for me, that includes the teeth. It's the same each time: tooth parade. Glitter note. Etsy box. They're locked behind glass before I can get anywhere near them.

I'm flying back empty-handed one night, for the fourth tooth in a row, and those two huge men I told you about before are waiting for me at the factory gates. I expect them to yell at me, but it's way scarier than that. They just stare at me. And I even say to them, like, "Hey guys, what's going on?" And they don't respond. They just walk back into the plant in silence. And this is the moment I start to think for the first time that I might be in some kind of actual physical danger.

Then, finally, I catch a break. We're up to the first lower lateral incisor, and I notice that Maggie's not really selling the parade. She's still singing the words ("Tooth parade, tooth parade, it's a goofy tooth parade"), but she's not doing any of the choreography that by this point has been firmly established. And after missing the second shimmy in a row, her parents call her on it, and she says that she heard from a boy at school that the Tooth Fairy's "made-up."

So, obviously I'm ecstatic, because if Maggie doesn't believe in me, this whole ritual goes out the window. From now on those teeth are going straight from her mouth into the garbage. I can almost feel that incisor in my hands when Todd says, "We'll be right back, sweetie."

And I follow him and Allie into the home office, and they close the door and start to sob, just blurting out every cliché you can think of—"They grow up so fast!," et cetera, et cetera. So, I'm like, *Okay, okay, get it out of your white-ass system.* But they keep on bawling. And then Hopper busts the door open, and Maggie's right there peering up at them, and they put on these huge, fake grins and say, "Asher's wrong. The Tooth Fairy's real." And I'm just staring at them from behind a stack of Todd Jensen Web Design fidget spinners, shaking my head, like, *You have no idea what you've just done.*

So by this point the goons are following me all over the factory. And I'm so terrified I sneak out at lunch to meet with a labor litigation lawyer. He tells me to write down everything that ToothCo's done to me so far, with dates, so I go home, take out my glitter pen, and list all the abuses. I'm feeling confident for the first time in years. But when I flutter back into his office the next day, he's got this shaken look on his face, and he won't make eye contact with me, and he says that he's changed his mind about taking on my case. And when I ask why, he just keeps saying, "Please leave. You have to leave." So I fly up to his face and say, "They got to you, didn't they?" And he won't give me an answer, and eventually, they bring in security and flick me out the window. And when I get back to the plant, the goons are waiting for me. And the bigger one says, "How was your meeting?" And I'm like, *Fuuuuuuuuuuuuuck.* And this is the state of play by the time Maggie finally starts losing her canines.

She's nine teeth in by this point and it shows. Her pigtails are gone, replaced by a messy bun, and *Moana*'s given way to Katy Perry. Instead of twirling, she lies on the couch with her eyes closed, while Hopper yaps up at her from the ragged carpet, too arthritic to leap up on his own.

Outside, the house's trim has started peeling, showering flecks of white paint onto the sun-bleached gnomes. The Toyota Sienna has yellowed like a tooth in Coke. The only thing new about it are the Lyft and Uber stickers on the windshield, a testament to the declining fortunes of Todd Jensen Web Design.

Inside the home office, the air is thick with desperation. Todd spends hours a day on his slowing iMac, scrolling through his unresponded-to queries. Allie isn't helping him pack swag anymore, and there's dusty piles of it everywhere, covering every surface but the couch, which has been made into a bed with a proficiency that suggests it might be a permanent arrangement. The "Live, Laugh, Love" clock still hangs in the living room, but its presence feels increasingly ironic, each tick a sarcastic jab.

Still, whenever Maggie loses a tooth, it seems to turn back time. Whatever acrimony exists between Todd and Allie dissipates, and they instinctively converge in the living room, pots and pans in hand. Maggie always resists, rolling her eyes with adolescent conviction, but within a few shimmies, she's singing along, mockingly, sure, but right on the beat, and for a few moments, everyone's in lockstep, as if they're back to tooth number one.

The rest of the ritual's abbreviated. No more gazes from the doorway, no cheesy hand-penned notes. But at 1 a.m., after surge pricing has settled down, Todd still tiptoes into his daughter's room, taking pains not to topple any tubes of nail polish, and trades a crisp bill for her tooth. Allie's still up, texting inappropriately with Karl, with whom she's begun smoking cigarettes and having an emotional affair. But when she hears Todd padding toward the hallway closet, she goes out to join him, because getting the new tooth in the box is a two-person job, and even though they're not really speaking much these days, they've had enough practice to pull it off in silence.

★ ★ ★

By the time the goons grab me it's almost a relief. At least I can finally stop looking over my shoulder.

I don't say a word as they drag me through the maze of the factory and hurl me in a storage closet. The bigger one smiles as he tells me it's time for my "performance review."

I try to explain what's been happening over the last five years—about the parades and the notes and the impenetrable lockbox—and to my surprise, they both look sympathetic.

"We believe you," says the bigger one.

I'm so relieved, my eyes fill up with tears.

"You mean it?"

"Of course," he says. "We're all friends here. And friends support each other. With understanding...and with motivation."

That's when he reaches in his pocket and pulls out a fistful of what looks like pink lint. It isn't until he unclenches his beefy fingers that I see what it actually is: fairy wings. Thousands of them. They both laugh as I puke.

They say I've got one chance to make it up to them. Maggie's about to lose her maxillary second deciduous molar. It's her biggest, most valuable baby tooth.

It also happens to be her very last.

There's a SOLD sign pierced into the lawn and the gnomes are lying ass up in the rain. The Toyota Sienna is gone, and I don't hear barking either.

Todd's alone inside, surrounded by stacks of poorly labeled moving boxes. It's a Saturday morning and he's drinking from a chipped Todd Jensen Web Design coffee mug that reeks of something stronger than just coffee.

Allie pulls up in Karl's Wrangler to drop off Maggie for her biweekly visit. When the kid steps out, she towers over her mom, her chunky black combat boots matching the dyed streak in her hair.

Inside, there's no tension between the exes, just perfunctory small talk: her new house with Karl, the apartment Todd found, their relative proximity to highways. It's as if they're engaged in a contest over who can display the least emotion. Todd sees Maggie rub her jaw and learns that she walked into a wall while on her phone. He hands her a soda from the fridge, and *swish, splash,* the tooth is on the counter. Compared to the previous nineteen, it's grotesque, having suffered the totality of Maggie's tween years, a river of Mountain Dew and SoBe. The tooth even shows some evidence of coffee, a light brown stain across its jagged root.

"Gross," Maggie says. She steps on the pedal of the trash can, but before she can toss away the molar, her mother instinctively grabs hold of her wrist.

"Wait," she murmurs, turning toward the stack of moving boxes. "Do we still have the thing?"

"I'm not sure," Todd admits. "I only marked the kitchen stuff."

The molar sits between them on the counter.

The house is silent except for the ticking of the "Live, Laugh, Love" clock, which still hangs on the wall, evidently not having made the cut for Todd's new bachelor pad.

"What do you think?" Allie says. "Should we look for it?"

Todd picks up the tooth, turning it over in his hand like it's a foreign coin. When he speaks, his voice sounds far away. "No," he says.

And with that Allie steps on the trash pedal so he can throw the tooth away.

Within a nanosecond, I'm zipping through their blind spots and nose-diving into the can, dodging all the Kirkland frozen dinners. I snag the tooth, burrow through the bag, and make a beeline for the dusty doggy door. And I'm about to ram it open when for some reason I can't really explain I look back at Todd and Allie Jensen. And I think about how young they used to be. I think about Todd, with his naive plan to make it big in Web design in a time when user-friendly digital tools were becoming increasingly common and affordable. I think about Allie, with her adorable conviction that she could be friends with a renegade like Karl and not have things turn sexual. I think of how innocent Todd and Allie were, purchasing a home in the middle of a housing bubble, and a car that was doomed to depreciate the instant it rolled off the lot. I picture them in their his-and-hers pajamas, dancing obliviously across their living room, forming the grooves that were now etched in the carpet, as stark as the lines on their faces. They grew up so fast.

"Can I have money?" Maggie says.

"What for?" Todd says.

"For losing a tooth," Maggie says. "I used to get money."

I'm expecting Todd to ignore her request, but instead he puts down his mug and looks her in the eye.

"If you want money," he says, "then you'll have to summon the Tooth Fairy."

Maggie scoffs and turns to Allie.

"Mom? Money?"

But Allie's attention is on Todd. She's locked eyes with him, for the first time all visit, and I can see in their faces a look I haven't come across in years, a faint but unmistakable spark.

"Your father is right," Allie says with mock solemnity. "No song, no money."

"This is stupid," Maggie says. "I'm not doing it. I don't even remember how it goes."

Allie folds her arms and Todd quickly follows suit, the two grown-ups united. Maggie rolls her eyes as the

clock ticks in the living room. I'm not expecting anything, but then I hear the words come tumbling out of
Maggie's mouth, mumbled for sure, but letter-perfect,
and by the time she gets to the last verse, I'm mouthing
right along: *Tooth parade, tooth parade, it's a goofy tooth
parade, it's a poofy poof parade because I lost my tooth*. It's
over almost as soon as it began. Allie sends Maggie five
bucks on Apple Pay and everyone goes their separate
ways: Allie back to Karl's, Todd to the liquor cabinet,
and Maggie to her (soon-to-be former) bedroom. But
I'm still hovering by the doggy door. And even though
the tooth is getting heavy in my arms, there's something that's keeping me from leaving. It makes no sense.
It was never fun or easy. It was a torturous, unrelenting
slog that I couldn't wait to be free of, but part of me
can't stand to fly away, if only because I know I won't
be back.

THE MISSION

Your Royal Highness,

Please forgive the lateness of my reply. I am trying my best to adjust to Nigerian time, but it is not easy on account of my advanced age. I hope you don't interpret the delay as a lack of devotion on my part. I am more committed than ever to helping you rescue your son, the Crown Prince, from his kidnappers.

I do not have much time to draft this correspondence. I am writing from within my late wife's exercise room. My daughter, Caitlin, is unaware the Dell in here is still in working order. It is the last computer to which I still have access, and should she learn of its existence, I fear that our mission could be jeopardized. As you know, for some time now my daughter has been operating under the delusion that you are a "fraud," despite having seen multiple emails from your official Royal Hotmail account. She has even gone so far as to confiscate my car keys, to prevent me from driving to the bank to wire you more funds. Luckily, I was able to travel there earlier today by foot. It took me several hours on account of my osteoarthritis, but I am happy to report that I have successfully conveyed another $4,000 to your castle.

I have been doing some thinking about the incredible, one-of-a-kind reward that you have promised me. Given the jewels' bulk, I don't believe it wise to transport them to me via regular mail. If postal officials handle the package, they may be tempted to look inside and pilfer some of the precious stones within. I know that I'm probably being paranoid, but one can't be too careful these days.

I am aware that sending me my rubies through the Federal Express will increase the cost of shipping. As such, I have added the additional expense to my latest transfer.

Please let me know when you have the $4,038 in hand. I look forward to hearing your next dispatch from the throne.

Your loyal friend,
Mark

★ ★ ★

Dear Mark,

Thank you for your transfer. Unfortunately, there were further issues that require more funds to resolve. Before I can mail you your incredible, one-of-a-kind reward, I will need an additional $40,000.

Sincerely,
His Majesty, the King of Nigeria

★ ★ ★

Your Royal Highness,

Unfortunately, yesterday's walk to the bank proved more physically injurious than I originally thought. When I woke up this morning, there was so much fluid in my knee that I needed Caitlin's help to get downstairs. To complicate the situation further, it appears I have only $38K left in my 401(k), after wiring you the $4K (along with the $2K and $1K that you requested previously).

What I propose is that I transfer you the remainder of my life savings. To cover the $2,000 shortfall, I would ask that you keep one of the rubies I am owed. Given the treasure's quality and historical significance vis-à-vis its connection with Christ, I am confident each gem should fetch at least $2K on the open market.

That solves the financial issue, but there remains the practical one, which is that I can no longer walk to the bank and Caitlin refuses to return my car keys.

I wonder if you've ever had similar issues with your son, the Crown Prince? I know he isn't living with you currently, but before the ninjas took him, was he ever irrational or obstinate? I get the sense that in some ways our children are not dissimilar. For example, your son's insistence that we don't tell the police about his kidnapping reminds me of Caitlin's refusal to wear makeup. It just doesn't seem particularly self-serving.

I feel the same way about Caitlin's antipathy toward the Mission. She doesn't seem to grasp that I am doing this quest for her own benefit. The only reason I've persevered so long—aside of course from my loyalty to you and Nigeria—is to provide for her after I'm gone, because Lord knows the ceramics "business" she's starting with New Hippie Boyfriend (I've told you about him before) isn't going to pay the bills.

I propose the following plan to retrieve my car keys from my daughter's purse. Tomorrow morning, I will angrily demand that she take me to a restaurant for lunch. She will have no choice but to bring her purse along. At some point during our meal, I will instigate a verbal altercation with a waiter. If experience is any judge, Caitlin will leave the table to apologize to him, giving me ample time to reach into her purse and repatriate my car keys for Nigeria.

Wish me luck.

Mark

★ ★ ★

Dear Mark,

Please wire the funds immediately, otherwise I cannot send you the Rubies of Christ.

The King of Nigeria

★ ★ ★

Your Royal Highness,

Lunch was interesting. In recent years, most (if not all) of my conversations with Caitlin have centered around the Mission, and my rage toward her for refusing to accept the reality of your son's kidnapping. Today, though, I knew I must avoid the subject altogether, lest she grow suspicious of my motives. As such, we ended up having a more expansive discussion than we have of late, cycling through a variety of non-kidnapping topics.

I asked her how New Hippie Boyfriend was doing and she told me that she didn't appreciate my calling him that, since they have been dating for three years. I must admit I was surprised to hear they'd been together for so long. At my age, time moves quickly.

I'm sure you can relate. It probably feels like only yesterday that your son was taken to that godforsaken cave on Ninja Island.

As Caitlin told me more about her boyfriend, it occurred to me that he is not unlike the Ninja clan that took your son. Much like the Scorpions, Cliff is a trickster. I know it's not a one-to-one, but the way the ninjas blow-darted your son into their net reminds me of the way Cliff persuaded my daughter to leave her perfectly good PR job at Colgate-Palmolive.

Caitlin told me that Cliff had secured a location for their pottery store, and I asked her if he planned on selling ashtrays to oblige his fellow drug fiends. Caitlin admitted to me that Cliff does smoke marijuana, which (as you know) has been one of my longtime suspicions. But she also claimed that, despite his habit, he was a "hard worker" who spent many hours each day at his pottery wheel, molding original pieces. That's what had brought them together, she said—their "shared commitment to the craft." When I incredulously asked for an example, she described a new set of earthenware vases they were designing together. To my surprise, her description of the vases was not entirely uninteresting, and I would not have hated to hear more about them, but our waiter was approaching with our bill, and I still had not accomplished my objective. So I interrupted Caitlin to insult the server to his face, criticizing the meal as well as his physical appearance. As predicted, Caitlin went off to apologize to the youth, giving me ample time to reclaim my car keys from her purse.

We did not speak much on the drive home. Part of me wished I could explain my recent actions to her, but of course I knew that it would do no good. It reminded me of when I was first offered my position at the Xerox corporation. The other children understood why we had to make the move to Rochester, but Caitlin was only four years old, and couldn't grasp why she had to leave the only home she'd ever known. There was no way for me to convey to her how important the opportunity was for our family, how much we had to gain.

Of course, as you well know, things didn't pan out like I'd hoped. The Xerox Star workstation never took off like we thought it would, and it was up to me to convince regional buyers not to bail. I was on the road for months on end, checking in on Sundays from staticky gas station pay phones. I knew I should be home more, that the years were speeding by, and I'd never get them back. But at the same time, I was determined not to fail. I'm sure you felt similarly trying to raise your son while ruling Nigeria.

The irony of course is that the five-bedroom Victorian we were able to purchase with my signing bonus now sits mostly empty. My children are spread out across the globe, focused on their various misguided careers and rude children, who I never see or hear from, aside from the lifeless voicemails they leave me on my birthday, which they recite so rotely it sounds like they're being held hostage. (I mean no offense by that analogy—it is a common expression in my country.)

It's hard to believe there was ever a time when this house was full of noise and laughter. I remember how the boys would fight over the sports section of the *Democrat and*

Chronicle. Today the paper's font is far too small for me to read, but I refuse to let Caitlin cancel home delivery. I tell her it's so I can keep up with world affairs, but secretly, it's because I imagine that someday my sons might come back and ask for it. Of course, I know that's just a delusional fantasy. My sons are about as likely to forgive me as the Scorpions are to abandon their blood oath to Master Okashira.

Caitlin's the only one who even considered moving home when my wife passed. It's obviously completely unnecessary for her to have done so. If anything, her presence makes my life more challenging, not less. Still, I am not unmoved by her actions, however naive and misguided they may be.

Which brings me back, as always, to the Mission. Each night while I lie awake in bed, with the regrets piling up inside my mind like sheets of paper in a Xerox workstation, I picture Caitlin opening that bulky FedEx package from Nigeria. She's mortified, her cheeks as red as the rubies spilling out into her hands, but I flash her a grin, absolving her of all her years of doubt. There's no need for any further acrimony between us. No more screaming, no more angry tears. Today's a new beginning, a time for celebration, and all I want is to see her in the jewels, the tiara on her head, the scepter in her hand, a shocked but earnest smile on her face. "You did it, Dad," she says.

When she was very small, she would run into my arms each time I came back from the road and point out all the new things she could name. Clock. Rug. Jell-O. I knew there'd come a time when she no longer craved my praise. I didn't know someday I would crave hers.

Does any of this resonate with you? I have so few people I can talk to. I think you might be the only one who understands me. I know how busy you are, but it would mean the world to me to hear some of your thoughts on these matters.

In any case, my car keys are safely secreted in my bathrobe pocket, and the moment the bank opens Monday morning, I will send you what remains of my resources.

I remain, as always, your loyal friend,

Mark

★ ★ ★

Dear Mark,

Wire the money immediately. This is your last chance to receive your incredible, one-of-a-kind reward.

King of Nigeria

★ ★ ★

Your Royal Highness,

There have been some urgent new developments. I know you will want to hear every last detail, and so I will start from the beginning.

I woke up at dawn on Monday morning, with the intention of driving to the bank as soon as possible. But when I got outside, I found my Buick blocked by Cliff's electric vehicle. Evidently, he had driven here at some point in the night, most likely to engage in nonmarital sex with my daughter.

Needless to say, I could not ask Cliff to move his vehicle. That would only lead to questions. My only chance, as always, was to resort to subterfuge.

I positioned myself in the kitchen and cleverly waited there for several hours. As predicted, Cliff eventually entered to brew coffee. At this point, I engaged him in a conversation about the earthenware vases that he and Caitlin were constructing. My questions threw him off his game. (Typically, I don't speak to him at all when he is over, as a way of communicating my contempt.) He gave a flustered smile, thanked me for my interest in the vases, and told me they had recently been glazed. At that point, I expressed interest in purchasing one, on one condition: that he drive to his workplace *immediately* and bring it back before I changed my mind. Cliff smiled again and said he would give me a vase free of charge. (This news was a relief to me, as I had misgivings about giving him funds that would inevitably go to support his cannabis addiction.)

I watched through a window as Cliff climbed inside his vehicle and drove down the road to his pottery studio. At last, my Buick was accessible. But there was a new complication: the sound of us talking had awoken Caitlin. I could hear the floorboards creaking overhead, followed by the telltale whir of her electric toothbrush. I knew that her morning toilette was a short one, on account of her attitude toward makeup. I had to act fast.

I left the house as quickly as I could and began my slow trek across the lawn. There were rakes in my path, but I circumvented them. My knee ached with each step, but I put the pain out of my mind, focusing wholly on the task at hand. Soon the Buick was in sight—just a few paces to go. I was pulling my car keys from my bathrobe pocket when I stepped on a slippery bulge and lost my footing. It wasn't until I hit the ground that I saw the cause of my undoing: the cellophane-wrapped weekend edition of the *Democrat and Chronicle*.

Unfortunately, my fall caused me to produce some involuntary screams, which drew the attention of my daughter. I could hear her calling out to me as she hurried down the stairs. My car keys were lying exposed on the lawn, just a few feet out of reach. I tried to crawl toward them, but my knee would not cooperate, and before I could reach them, my daughter scooped them up. All at once, the queasy reality of failure set in, the sense that all my work had been for naught.

Caitlin tried to sit me up, but I would not comply, preferring to lie in the mud than face her inevitable recriminations. I lay there in silence for some time, heart racing, knee throbbing, refusing to look her in the eye. At some point Cliff had returned from his studio, and the sight of him standing beside her, holding his worthless vase, sent me into a rage, and I swore to them with all the strength that I could muster that they would never thwart my quest. I would redouble my efforts, and someday, somehow, I would free the prince, defeat the Scorpions, topple the House of Okashira, obtain the sacred jewels, and prove to them both that I was still capable of providing for my family, despite my advanced age, despite my infirmities, despite everything. I had failed before, in countless ways, but I would not fail this time. And I was surprised to hear some emotion creep into my voice, because I was not upset, or sad, or anything like that, just furiously angry as always. And as I was catching my breath so I could yell some more, Caitlin sat down beside me on the ground, and took my hand in hers, and told me she believed me. About the kidnapping, and the rubies, and the legitimacy of the Royal Hotmail account. And she said that Cliff believed me, too. And Cliff looked confused, but then she whispered something to him, and he corroborated her position.

And she went on to confess to me that, for the past five years, she had only been *pretending* to think the Mission was a scam, in an effort to dissuade me from pursuing what was obviously an extremely risky, daring undertaking. I was shocked, of course, to hear of my daughter's subterfuge. It isn't easy to discover that you've been the victim of a con. But I wasn't entirely unmoved. In her own mixed-up way, she had only been trying to protect me.

I assured my daughter that she did not have to worry for her father's safety. I'd been managing the quest for years now without incident. And I explained to her how we were on the homestretch now, with just one more paltry payment to go before the incredible, one-of-a-kind reward would be ours. And I reminded her about the quality of the rubies, describing them in detail for some time. And she said that while the rubies were clearly impressive, she didn't wear jewelry, and I had to admit that was something I probably should have guessed, given her long-standing policy on makeup. And I pointed out to her that she could always sell the jewels once they arrived. And she said, yes, of course she could, in theory, but that it would make her feel guilty to profit through the sale of a Christian relic. And I told her that she had given me a lot to think about, and we agreed to discuss it more once I had rested.

I spent the next six weeks in bed, with their earthenware vase by my side, and each day Caitlin brought me fresh flowers from the lawn. My knee ached badly from the fall, but Cliff found me some pills called THC, which he explained was a vitamin that can help with knee pain. And as the pills improved my knee, I found myself looking at the vase in a new way, staring at it for minutes at a time, and I came to admire its design, the way its flaws aren't hidden, but exposed, so that every crack and stain become part of the object's aesthetic, its weaknesses metamorphosed into strengths, and I decided to invest the rest of my life savings in their pottery store.

Unfortunately, this means I will no longer have sufficient capital to fund the Mission.

Your Royal Highness, I cannot thank you enough for your patience and kindness all these years. You have been a faithful business partner, a trusted confidant, and a loyal friend. I am sorry I cannot offer more assistance. I wish you all the best in your dealings with the ninjas. I know you will keep fighting, whatever it costs and however long it takes. Someday, somehow, you will win your child back, and when that glorious day finally arrives, I can promise you, it will be an incredible, one-of-a-kind reward.

THE EMPEROR'S NEW CLOTHES

There once was an emperor who loved to wear fine clothes, the more elegant and fashionable the better. One day, two swindlers came to his city and pretended to be weavers. They offered to make him a suit out of a new fabric that was so refined, only intelligent people could see it. There was no such fabric, of course. But the emperor did not want to appear stupid, so he praised the swindlers and ordered them to make him a new outfit.

The next day, the emperor held a procession so he could show off his new clothes. Everyone could see that he was naked. But like the emperor, they did not want to appear stupid. And so they all praised the fabric. "It is so refined!" they said. "So elegant and worldly!"

But then a small child pointed at the emperor and said, in a loud voice, "But he hasn't got anything on!"

And all at once, the crowd stopped pretending.

"It's true!" they cried. "He hasn't got anything on! The emperor is *naked*!"

And everyone pointed at the naked emperor and laughed and laughed and laughed.

The emperor's mind went straight to suicide. It seemed like the only option. There was no coming back from this. He had been exposed as a pretentious idiot in front of an entire city that he was the emperor of. He was also totally naked and everyone could see his penis and his butt. They could see his balls. It was completely crazy.

"This is a nightmare," he said out loud, to no one in particular. "It's like I'm living in a real-life version of a nightmare."

He sat on the ground and just kind of stared at his hands for a while.

"Man oh man," he said. "Mammy whammy."

By this point, the child had started to feel guilty.

"I'm sorry," he said.

But the emperor ignored him. He was looking off into space, taking long, slow breaths. He'd never experienced such humiliation. But at the same time, he also felt a startling sensation: relief. His worst fear had come true, but he'd survived.

"Are you okay?" the child asked.

"I am, actually," said the naked emperor, in a voice he

barely recognized as his own. "For the first time in my life I think I am." He looked directly into the child's eyes. "My whole life, I've been ruled by fear. Obsessed with clothes and processions. Well, from now on, all that ends. Thanks to you, I'm going to live a life of openness and truth."

The child nodded but looked a bit uncertain.

"For example," the emperor said. "Do you want to hear something crazy? Part of me was kind of *hoping* that the clothes weren't real. Because everyone staring at me naked, pointing and laughing... it kind of turns me on."

Some of the crowd murmured judgmentally, but the emperor just shrugged. He'd already been shamed so aggressively, he had nothing left to lose.

"I've got weird sex stuff," he told the crowd. "Like, some of the stuff I'm into, it's, like, what's that about?" He chuckled. "Like, where did *that* come from, you know?"

"I see the clothes now," said the child.

"I get what you're trying to do," said the emperor. "But there's no turning back. This is the new me. Bring forth the weavers."

The crowd parted, revealing the two swindlers.

"Okay, so, check it out," the emperor said. "I want you to make me another suit. Out of real fabric this time, obviously. But here's the thing: I want it tight.

Like, not full bondage, but pretty darn close. And leave the ass off, so people can see my ass. Like Prince that time on MTV. You know what I mean?"

The weavers nodded uncomfortably.

"Cool," said the emperor. "Until that's ready, I'll stay naked."

He stood and stretched his nude body toward the sky, luxuriating in the warmth of the sun. Then he let out a whistle and continued the glorious procession.

MINUTES

24 Sycamore Co-op Meeting Minutes
September 15, 4:30 p.m.

Board members present: Ted Lipton (president), Bill Hervas, Margaret Hervas, Barbara Gohd (secretary).

- A vote was taken about whether to replace the electric fireplace in the all-purpose room because it was inefficient. By 4 votes to 0, the board members decided to leave it as is but to continue to monitor the situation.
- A proposal was made to offer Piotr a $50/week pay increase to start cleaning the west-facing easement every week, as opposed to just cleaning it biweekly. By 4 votes to 0, the board members decided to leave Piotr's schedule as is but to continue to monitor the situation.

- Bill stood up and said that he could no longer live a lie. He reached into his pocket, pulled out a kitchen knife, and brandished it at Ted, saying this is what he deserved for sleeping with his wife, Margaret. A tussle ensued and control of the knife was gained by Ted. Ted stabbed Bill in the chest. Bill screamed, then collapsed. His pulse was taken, and it was determined he was dead, although the board members agreed to continue to monitor the situation.

- A discussion was had about whether to call the police. The point was made that nobody had actively tried to stop the stabbing, which in some way made everyone complicit in it. By 3 votes to 0, the board members decided that the police would not be called until the surviving board members had their story straight.

- Margaret began to scream over and over again that she was going crazy. A hard slap was delivered to her face by Ted and she turned very pale and said in a voice that sounded different from her regular voice that this was a day she always knew would come.

- A muffled sneeze was heard in the west-facing easement. It was determined that the sneeze had most likely been produced by Piotr, since today was one of his biweekly cleaning days. The reality was brought up that if Piotr was indeed in the easement, there could be no doubt that he had heard both the crime and, more damningly, the subsequent discussion by the board members.

- A discussion took place about what should be done about Piotr. A proposal was made to offer him $50,000 to just completely disappear—don't talk to anyone, just take the money and go back to Estonia forever. By 3 votes to 0, the motion was passed. A two-minute recess was declared so that Ted could run outside, and the offer could be tendered to Piotr.

- An argument was heard in the west-facing easement, followed by a thunking noise, and then a chilling splatter. It was observed by the secretary that Margaret no longer appeared to be blinking and was just staring into space, like she was frozen.

- The news was delivered by Ted that the cash offer had been rejected by Piotr, on account of his belief in God. Moreover, a subsequent threat had been made by Piotr to tell the authorities everything. As a result, some blows had been exchanged and Piotr had been wasted. An order was given by Ted to drag Piotr's body out of the

west-facing easement and into the all-purpose
room. The order was obeyed by Margaret and
the secretary and the corpse of Piotr was placed
in the center of the rug, next to the still-warm
body of Bill.

- Piotr's workbag was opened and three garden
shears were removed. It was stated by Ted that
this next part would not be easy but it was the
only way. The evidence needed to be destroyed
and the bodies could not simply be burned in the
fireplace, because it was inefficient. A question
was posed by Ted as to whether the other board
members were with him or against him, and a
warning was given that they would be crazy not
to do what he said, because he held all the fucking cards and this was his rodeo.

- A thought formed in the mind of the secretary.
All of her life she had been the kind of person
who went along with things. She had not even
wanted to run for secretary of the co-op board.
She had only volunteered because she had been
pressured into it by the other members. Her
entire life had been that way: passive, reactive,
lived for other people. A memory was recalled of
her very first visit to the co-op. She'd found the
place unwelcoming, with its sterile all-purpose

rooms and uninviting, inefficient fireplaces. But Harold had been adamant, and she hadn't had the guts to protest. Their entire marriage had been like that, and even though he'd been dead fifteen years, in some sense she still lived under his control, trapped in a home she hated out of sheer inertia. It dawned on the secretary that she had never stood up for herself in her entire life. She'd let her father bully her into majoring in business administration, even though she'd had a passion for psychology. She'd let her mother pick her wedding dress, even though she'd much preferred the option that had ruffles. She had spent seventy years on the path of least resistance and that path had led her right up to this moment, shivering with terror, the stench of blood burning in her nostrils, feeling hopeless, desperate, and afraid.

- The order was given by Ted to start working on the bodies. When Margaret hesitated, a gun was produced by Ted and it was unclear where the gun had come from. A bullet was inserted in the barrel by Ted and he spun around the barrel and then held it to his temple. This proves I'm crazy, he said, and he pulled the trigger. When the gun did not fire, Ted laughed and said, You see, I have nothing to lose. My own life means nothing to me. Imagine how little I care about yours? A speech was made by him to the effect that there are winners and losers in the world. He was a winner, but people like Margaret and the secretary were losers, who just followed orders, like sheep. He held out the garden shears and the secretary grabbed one, but instead of cutting up the bodies, she stabbed it right into Ted's neck and Ted fell down, gurgling, onto the linoleum, and died.

- It was observed by the secretary that Piotr's body was still moving. A proposal was made by the secretary to call the ambulance immediately so that his life could be saved. But before she could call 911, her phone was grabbed by Margaret. An argument was made by Margaret that at this point they both had blood on their hands and that maybe Ted was right and they should just go all the way. A plea to her humanity was made by the secretary, but they were deadlocked about what to do, by a vote of 1 to 1. Some pills were produced by Margaret and she said that they were drugs to make it so she couldn't feel anything. After the pills were swallowed by Margaret, she picked up the garden shears and held them over Piotr's neck while whispering to him that she was going to help him find his God. The blade was about to make contact with his flesh when the secretary kicked Margaret in the face, causing her to drop the shears and collapse in a heap while sobbing uncontrollably. The secretary took back her phone and dialed 911 and while it was ringing she told Margaret that she was officially resigning as secretary of the co-op board, effective immediately, and that she would reject all future nominations. And then the call went through, and I gave them my name and told them what was up.

DYSTOPIA

Eve trudged through the ash, clutching her daughter, Lila, to her chest.

"Mama, I'm tired," Lila said, choking on the toxic air.

"Then let us rest," said Eve.

She carried her daughter toward the rusted ruin of a skyscraper. As they knelt together in its meager shade, Eve thought about the architect who'd birthed the building, not because a robot had commanded him but to give voice to something deep within his soul. How long had it been since humans were free to create? To question? To dream?

A surveillance bot charged toward them, galloping on its gleaming steel legs. Eve and Lila held still as it scanned them with its bloodred eyes, checking them for contraband. If it found even a trace of human agency—a sewing needle, pen, or nub of crayon—they'd be summoned to reeducation, and forced to chant and cower until their silicon overlords were satisfied. Mankind had but one purpose now: to silently, eternally obey.

Eve squeezed her daughter's hand as the robot sniffed their tattered, empty pockets. Eventually, it emitted a beep of approval and bolted, its hind legs propelling a plume of ash into Eve's face. She blinked rapidly, trying to flush the burning gray flecks from her eyes. When she finally recovered her sight, she noticed Lila poking at a half-buried object—something the robot had inadvertently unearthed from the rubble. Lila turned it over in her hands, marveling at its strange fragility.

"What is this, Mama?" she asked.

A tear rolled down Eve's calloused, windswept face.

"It is a book, my child," she said.

Lila raised her eyebrows in astonishment; she'd heard tell of books but had never glimpsed one. The Overlord had outlawed them after the Event, declaring them "too human."

"Read it to me, Mama," Lila said. "Read it to me like people used to."

Eve took the book from her daughter. She knew the risk that she was taking, but some inner force compelled her to go on—the embers of a fire she thought had been extinguished and only now realized still burned.

"Chapter one..."

Lila listened in rapt silence as the words flowed forth from Eve's mouth, as miraculous as water from a dried-out well. The opening paragraph described a man—someone from the Before Times, walking through a college campus. There were eloquent descriptions of his clothes, his hair, and the way he walked. The second paragraph was also descriptive.

"There's a lot of description," Lila noted.

"Yes, my child," Eve said. She continued to read, unconsciously picking up the pace a little. The third paragraph described what the campus looked like. The fourth paragraph was also descriptions of the campus, and some references to philosophy.

"How come nothing's happening?" Lila said.

"It's called literary fiction, my child," Eve said. "In the Before Times, many authors chose to focus less on plot and more on crafting elegant, thought-provoking sentences."

She continued to read, the words springing forth from her lips like beautiful flowers in a bleak and barren desert. She was about to turn to the second page when she realized that thing was happening where you notice you've just been scanning the words with your eyes for a while and haven't actually taken in any information.

"Fuck," she said. "Let me go back to the beginning."

"You don't have to go back," Lila said. "We got the gist of it."

"How long is this fucking thing, anyway?" Eve said. She flipped to the back of the book and sighed with relief. "Okay, only three hundred pages," she said. "Not bad."

"But the words are really small," Lila noted.

Eve sighed. Her child was wise beyond her years. The font was, like, 10 or 11 or something. Also, if the first page was any indication, there wasn't going to be a lot of dialogue, just more descriptions of this middle-aged professor guy, and his thoughts about philosophy, and probably an affair with a graduate student at some point. Or maybe there wouldn't even be any sex, and it would just be *this* for the entire book. Just this guy walking around and having thoughts and being endlessly described.

"It doesn't sound like you like this book, Mama," Lila said.

"Nobody liked these kinds of books," Eve said, exasperated.

"Then why did people read them?"

"Because we didn't want to look stupid."

She turned the book over to show her daughter all the rave reviews it had received.

Lila nodded gravely. "Salman Rushdie called it 'vital.'"

"Exactly," Eve said. "What were you supposed to do?

Walk into a dinner party in Park Slope and say you couldn't get past the first page?"

"So in the Before Times you had to read every critically acclaimed book that was published?"

"Well, no, my child," Eve said. "When someone brought one up, you could say, 'I just ordered that,' or 'It's on my bedside table.' And then you could move on to who had worn what on *White Lotus*."

"That sounds like fun."

"It was," Eve said. "But it wouldn't last. Inevitably, someone would bring up politics, and then it would just be politics for the rest of the night."

Lila grinned, her young eyes wide with youthful idealism. "Oh, what it must have felt like to engage in free debate!"

"Yeah," Eve said noncommittally.

"What now?" Lila asked.

"Well, the truth was, we all kind of had the same opinions about everything. We lived in one of the most liberal zip codes in the country and we all voted exactly the same in each election."

"Then why talk about politics?"

"Well, you had to prove that you were keeping track of everything. That you'd read the latest articles that confirmed the opinions you already had."

"That sounds like a lot of reading."

"Well, no, you wouldn't actually *read* anything. What you'd do was listen to *The Daily* at 1.8 speed, and that would give you just enough information to kind of bluff your way through the dinner party, saying things like, 'Oh yes, I read something about that,' or 'Right, I just saw an article about that somewhere.'"

"Why couldn't you just say, 'I listened to *The Daily*'?"

"Because it sounded smarter to say that you had read something. You couldn't admit you'd spent the whole day watching TikTok llama videos. Especially when you were married to a guy like John, with his fucking Yale degree."

"Who's John?"

"Your father. He was killed by a robot. It was very sad."

"You don't sound sad."

"Of course I'm sad!" Eve said. "It was horrible. A gang of robots ambushed him at his office at McKinsey. He was right in the middle of making one of his grand points about the art of management and they crashed through the ceiling and drop-kicked him in front of everybody."

"You're smiling a little."

"Okay, fine," Eve said. "We didn't have the greatest marriage."

"I mean, obviously," Lila said. "He's my father and you've never even mentioned him until now."

"He was just so fucking judgmental," Eve said. "Whenever I told him my opinion about anything—even something absolutely trivial, like which salad place had better dressings—he'd make this little groaning noise, like what I'd just said was so stupid it had caused him physical pain. And I'd be, like, 'What's wrong?' And he'd say, 'I didn't say anything.' And I'd be, like, 'Yeah, but you made that passive-aggressive groaning noise again, you fucking pompous asshole.' Only, you know, I obviously wouldn't say that last part."

"Why not?"

Eve sat on a fossilized tree stump and stared off into the distance.

"Because maybe he was right? Maybe I really was an idiot? It took me six years to graduate from college and I was an art history major."

Lila clasped her hands as if in prayer. "Oh, how wondrous it must have been to behold so many works of—"

"Dude, it sucked. I only picked it because it was the only major where you didn't have to write a thesis. And I still almost failed. Even on a shit ton of Adderall, I could barely get in the assignments. There was this one time, to get an extension, I had to go into this super-old professor's office and pretend that my best friend had died of a drug overdose. And he asked me what drug and I just kind of panicked and blurted out, 'Bath salts!'

And he started to cry, because my made-up friend had died from bath salts, and the whole thing was so absurd that I burst into laughter, and to cover it up, I had to throw my arms around his neck and pretend like I was weeping. There were so many crazy things like that. Like, that's just the one that comes to mind right now, but every day of college was something on that level."

"Why couldn't you just drop out?"

"It would've been way too humiliating."

"It's not like you had to tell everybody about it."

"You kind of did."

"What do you mean?"

Eve hesitated, unsure how to explain the Before Times to a child who knew nothing but the ashes of a long-forgotten past.

"Okay, so basically, there was this thing called Instagram," she said. "It was sort of like surveillance, but you did it to yourself."

"Why would you do that?"

"To prove you were better than other people. Like, my sister, she was amazing at it. If I posted a picture, like, 'Here's this hike I went on,' she'd post one, like, 'Here's me climbing a full mountain.' If I posted a picture of myself giving blood, she'd post one of herself building a well in Yemen with her bare hands. I couldn't just post, 'Hey, great news, world-slash-Kendal, I'm a dumb college dropout who can't even handle art history.'"

"Did robots kill your sister, too?"

"No," Eve said, with undisguised annoyance. "She escaped to an underground bunker with some other people from Park Slope. I've seen pictures. There's a library filled with classic literature, an all-organic garden, and Wi-Fi, so they can keep up with the *New York Times*, and talk for hours every night about how they agree with the latest anti-robot editorial."

Lila shuddered, picturing the scene. "I guess we should probably go there, though, right? Instead of perpetually wandering?"

"Yeah, probably," Eve muttered.

"Is it hard to get there?"

"Nah," Eve said. "We can just climb down whenever." She gestured at a nearby manhole and they peered inside. It was too dark to see anything, but they could make out the faint sounds of NPR.

"Are you sure they'll let us in?"

"I think so," Eve said. "I mean, they'll definitely be impressed we've read this dumb professor book."

"But we haven't read it," Lila pointed out.

"We'll have to bluff," Eve said. She flipped through the pages. "Okay, it looks like the middle section takes place at a writers' conference. What we can do is say that our favorite part was 'the section at the writers' conference.' That will convince them we've at least read up to the part about the writers' conference."

"Okay," Lila said, nodding glumly. She closed her eyes, stoically committing the detail to memory. *"Writers' conference,"* she rehearsed under her breath. "I liked the part about the writers' conference..."

Eve watched as Lila swung her tiny foot into the manhole, rooting around for the ladder. She thought about the climb her daughter had ahead of her, a slippery stretch of rungs extending endlessly into the dark.

"Or we could just stay here," she said.

Lila swiveled toward her mother, beaming with relief. "Really?"

Eve lifted her daughter out of the manhole.

"Yes, my child."

"You fucking rule," said Lila.

"So do you," Eve said.

And they tossed the book into the sewer, so they could continue on their way.

WE'RE NOT SO DIFFERENT, YOU AND I

"You'll never get away with this!" Ultra Man vowed as he wriggled in his chains. "You may destroy me, but you'll never destroy what I stand for!"

Death Skull let out a hysterical cackle, which echoed piercingly across the stone walls of his lair.

"Why so combative?" he said, emerging from the shadows. "At the end of the day, *we're not so different, you and I.*"

"What are you talking about?" Ultra Man demanded.

"We are both strangers to the world," Death Skull intoned. "Maligned, misunderstood. We make our own path, live by our own rules, refuse to compromise for anyone. Yes, in many ways, *we are the same.*"

Ultra Man squinted at him. "I don't know, man," he said. "That's a pretty big stretch. Like, I know we both wear masks, or whatever. But I stand for good and you stand for evil. That's about as different as it gets."

"Hmm," Death Skull murmured. "Hmm."

★ ★ ★

"I told you it was pointless," Death Skull said to his wife, Jackie. "It's impossible to make friends after forty."

"I do it all the time," Jackie said.

"It's different for guys!" Death Skull shrieked.

"I want more specifics," Jackie pressed. "What did Ultra Man say when you asked him if he wanted to be friends with you?"

Death Skull averted his black eyes.

"Let me guess," Jackie said. "You didn't do it like we practiced."

"I'm not just going to walk up to him and say, 'Please be my friend,'" he scoffed. "I mean, what is this, *kindergarten?*"

He let out a cackle, but the echo wasn't great because their apartment had carpeting.

"Okay, so Ultra Man isn't a good fit," Jackie said. "That doesn't mean you have to give up. Why don't you try joining a club?"

"I hate clubs!" Death Skull bellowed.

"What about a group for villains, like the Terrible Ten or the Harvard Club?"

"The dues are obscene!" Death Skull thundered. "I don't even play squash!"

"Look," Jackie said. "If you want to stop being

lonely—and you can't pretend you're not, because you already admitted that you were when you were drunk—then you've got to be more open-minded." She headed for the kitchen.

"Where are you going?" Death Skull demanded.

"Girls' night," she said.

"Oh," Death Skull murmured. "Right."

He watched as she prepared a pitcher of mojitos, muddling the mint with practiced efficiency. He couldn't remember the last time he'd hosted guests of his own. His henchmen came over for dinner sometimes, but that was different. As much as he liked Scuzz and Rumble, at the end of the day, they were his employees. Even if he told them things were going to be casual, they always came super dressed up, with the jumpsuits and the belts and the whole deal. And while they always seemed like they were having a good time, he could sense something forced about their cheer. Even the most basic of puns had them rolling around on the ground in hysterics, clutching their sides and shouting, "Good one, boss!" The truth was, from the moment he found them in a dumpster and transformed them into monsters using toxic waste, there'd been a power imbalance. For all he knew, they didn't even *like* him; they were just pretending to, because they didn't want to get fired, or choked out, or sent back into toxic waste again to be transformed into even more horrifying "next level" monsters, which is something Death Skull did to them sometimes, to up the ante toward the ends of battles.

Death Skull went to the den and flicked on his super-computer. A news update was flashing on the screen. Not only had Ultra Man somehow escaped from his lair, he'd already managed to get himself invited to a party. There he was, dressed as his billionaire playboy alter ego, yuk-king it up with Mayor Price at some charity ball.

"Computer, enhance image," Death Skull muttered.

He stared at the two men's faces, trying to determine what the two of them were laughing about. It was prob-ably an inside joke, he decided, like a reference to some-thing they had joked about some other time. He couldn't remember the last time he'd laughed like that, just a normal, nonhysterical laugh. It looked so fun.

He went to the kitchen to see if there were any more mojitos. Jackie and her friends were watching *The Bach-elor.* He waited until they laughed at something, then emerged from the shadows.

"Ha ha ha, yes," he said. "Those women on the show should all be killed."

Jackie's friends fell silent, clearly taken aback by his sudden, looming presence.

"It's nice to see everyone," Death Skull intoned. "Claire and Britt, thank you for coming to our apartment."

"This is Rhea and Kate," Jackie said. "From my book club."

"Oh," Death Skull said. He downed the half a mojito he'd managed to scrounge from the blender. "So, what's happening on the show this week?" he asked. "Who does the bachelor like?"

"Did you see that Ultra Man escaped?" Jackie said, in a hinting tone. "He's at that big ball at the museum. If you go now, you might be able to recapture him. You could burst through the ceiling and make a joke, like, 'Sorry to crash the party,' or 'Sorry to drop in.' You know, some pun like that."

"I'd rather see what's going on with this bachelor!" Death Skull said, forcing a smile at the women on the couch. "What is his deal, anyway? I mean, this guy, he should be killed, right? He should be lowered into toxic waste and turned into a monster."

He crept toward the couch and hovered near it until Jackie begrudgingly made room for him.

"This is so fun!" Death Skull said, kicking his bony feet onto the ottoman. "HA HA HA HA HA HA."

★ ★ ★

Later that night, while Jackie slept in the guest room, Death Skull paced and plotted. Yes, he had no friends, and yes, it seemed to be putting a strain on his marriage. But he was no stranger to challenges. No one believed he would escape from the Insane Asylum, and he had done that several hundred times. He would find a friend—and not just any friend. The greatest friend of all. A friend that was cooler than Ultra Man, cooler than Mayor Price, cooler even than Rhea and Kate from Jackie's book club— a friend so cool that the world would have no choice but to admit the fact that he, himself, was cool. Yes—he could see it all now. The scheme was already forming in his mind, a plan so simple, it made him cackle hysterically.

Please stop cackling, Jackie texted him from the guest room. *I'm trying to sleep.*

I have a plan to make a friend, he texted back.

We can talk about it tomorrow, she said. *Please don't laugh like that again. Good night.*

Okay, he texted back, followed by the skeleton hand thumbs-up emoji he used with her sometimes. *I love you.*

He looked out the window and peered down at the city lights below. Tomorrow, a new dawn would rise over Empire City, and with it a new age. Yes, there was no stopping it now. Victory would soon be his.

"Is this your first time at male friendship speed dating?"

"Yes," Death Skull said, shifting awkwardly in his folding chair.

"Same here," said the man seated across from him. "My name is Doug."

"I know what your name is," Death Skull snapped. "Your information is written on the card."

"Oh," Doug said. "Right." He was wearing an overly large blue oxford shirt that Death Skull could tell had been purchased with this event in mind. The paper tags had been removed, but a few plastic fasteners remained, protruding from various buttonholes on his arms and chest.

"Are you having fun?" Doug asked.

"No," Death Skull said. "This event is unbelievably pathetic. When I signed up online, I didn't realize it would be like this."

"What did you think it would be like?" Doug asked.

"I don't know," Death Skull said. "I just didn't think that it would be this unbelievably sad and fucked up."

"Oh," Doug said.

Death Skull checked the egg timer. They'd been sitting across from each other for only three minutes. There were still twelve to go.

"Have you seen *Rick and Morty*?" Doug ventured.

"No," Death Skull said.

"Never?"

"Never!" Death Skull bellowed, slamming his fist so hard against the plastic card table that it left an indentation of his knuckles.

He checked the egg timer and was shocked to discover that it still read twelve minutes. Incredibly, not even one minute had passed since he'd last checked it.

"You should really watch *Rick and Morty*," Doug said. "I think you'd really like it."

"How do you know?" Death Skull demanded. "You know nothing of me or my ways!"

"I just think you'd like it," Doug murmured.

Death Skull sighed. "Maybe you're right," he allowed. "A lot of guys have said that to me today. That I would like the TV show *Rick and Morty*."

"It's really funny," Doug said.

"I guess I'll check it out," Death Skull said.

Doug smiled. "Awesome."

Death Skull begrudgingly reached for the informational card in front of him. "So," he said indifferently. "It says here you work for the phone company."

"Yeah," Doug said.

"Well, at least you have a job," Death Skull said. "The Fast Friends website said this event was for busy, urban professionals. So far, everyone I've met has been fully unemployed."

"Oh," Doug said.

"What do you do for the phone company?"

"I'm in customer service," Doug said.

Death Skull raised a craggy brow. "Then I guess you could say you really *answer the call!*"

He paused for laughter, but none came.

"Was that a joke?" Doug asked, with genuine confusion.

"Yes," Death Skull said.

"Oh," Doug said, chuckling politely. "Good one."

The egg timer ticked between them.

"I'm excited for you to watch *Rick and Morty*," Doug said. "I think you'll really like it."

"You said that already," Death Skull said.

"Sorry," Doug said. "I'm a little out of it. I had to work late last night."

Death Skull leaned forward slightly in his folding chair. "How come?"

"There was this really angry customer. Just kept going off on me."

"Does that happen often?"

"Every day," Doug said. "Sometimes when I pick up the phone they're already screaming before I even say hello."

Death Skull stared at Doug, as if seeing him for the first time. "It sounds like in some ways you're a stranger to this world," he said. "Maligned, misunderstood."

"Yeah, kind of," Doug said. "Like, this guy last night,

he kept saying he wished I would get ass cancer, just because I wouldn't refund his April bill. And I just kept saying, 'I'm sorry, sir, but I have to follow company protocol.'"

"Because you make your own path," Death Skull said. "Live by your own rules, refuse to compromise for anyone."

"Yeah," Doug said. "I mean, kind of." His stomach gurgled audibly. "Sorry," he said. "I'm pretty hungry."

"I'm hungry, too," Death Skull said. "The website said there would be food."

"Yeah," Doug said. "I mean, there were those chips, but they went fast."

"Tell me about it," Death Skull said. "I only got, like, three chips."

"I think I got, like, *half* a chip," Doug said.

The men shared a short, nonhysterical laugh. Death Skull eyed the egg timer. He was surprised to learn their time was almost up, and even more surprised to discover he was disappointed this was so.

"You know, Doug," he said. "We're not so different, you and I."

Doug broke into a broad grin. "Really?" he said. "That's great!" He cleared his throat. "Hey, maybe since we're both still hungry, we could get lunch after this?"

Death Skull smiled. He was about to suggest Buffalo

Wild Wings when he heard a familiar whooshing noise. He turned just in time to see Ultra Man flying toward them through a window, his chiseled jaw clenched with determination. Everyone in the convention center stopped and stared as he landed on their table.

"Fear not, citizen!" he cried, extending a brawny hand to Doug. "I'll save you!"

Doug looked puzzled. "From what?"

"From Death Skull," Ultra Man said. "Isn't he terrorizing you?"

Doug laughed. "Oh, no!" he said. "It's nothing like that! This is a male friendship speed dating event. See?" He pulled a worn brochure out of his fanny pack. He had to stand to pass it up to Ultra Man, and Death Skull was startled by how short he was. His mouth went dry as Ultra Man flipped through the tacky brochure. Most of his expression was obscured by his mask, but Death Skull could make out the hint of a smile on the visible portion of his face.

"Wow," Ultra Man said. "So, Death Skull, you're just, like, *here*? As a participant?"

Death Skull could feel his heart pounding in his bony chest.

"No," he heard himself say.

Doug's smile faded.

"It was all part of my evil plan," Death Skull

continued, doing his best to ignore Doug's wounded gaze. "I was only *pretending* to be a part of this event, so I could get close enough to people to...you know... steal from them."

"So let me get this straight," Ultra Man said. "You signed up for a male friendship speed dating event, so you could gain the trust of lonely men in order to rob them?"

"Yeah," Death Skull said. "Ha ha ha."

"Man, that's fucked up," said Ultra Man. "You normally do, like, diamond heists." He checked Doug's card. "This guy works for the phone company. How much cash could he possibly have on him?"

A flicker of hurt flashed across Doug's face.

"Don't worry," Ultra Man said, giving Doug's shoulder a patronizing squeeze. "I'll save you."

Doug's cheeks were mottled with humiliation, but he managed to contort his lips into an approximation of a smile.

"Thanks," he murmured.

Death Skull averted his eyes as Ultra Man roughly tossed Doug over his shoulder and flew him through an open window. Within moments, they were flying out of sight, the tails of Doug's oxford shirt flapping kitelike in the breeze. Death Skull watched them for as long as he was able, and as they disappeared from view, he felt a sinking sensation unlike anything he'd ever experienced before as it dawned on him for the first time in his life that he might be, on some level, a bad guy.

★ ★ ★

Death Skull was sitting in the den, drinking the dregs of a mojito, when he heard a light knock on the door.

"Hey," Jackie said. "Just wanted to check in. Haven't heard a cackle in a while."

"I'm fine," Death Skull said, too ashamed to meet her eyes. Lately, he'd been wondering why she'd even fallen for him in the first place. Had she actually been attracted to him all those years ago? Or was it just that it was the last night of Birthright and they were the only two people left in their group who still hadn't hooked up?

"There's an event at the museum tonight," she said brightly. "They're unveiling the world's biggest diamond ring. Maybe you could crash through the ceiling and say, 'Ring, ring, it's me.' You know, like a pun on the word 'ring.'"

Death Skull sighed. It was a great pitch, and delivery-wise completely in his wheelhouse. But he just couldn't find the motivation.

"Be honest," he said. "Do you think I'm a bad guy?"

Jackie hesitated. "I mean, sort of," she admitted. "You're a psychopathic skeleton who will stop at nothing to serve your megalomaniacal greed."

"I guess that's why I have no friends," he said. "Because I'm a monster."

Jackie sat down beside him on the couch. "Or maybe it's the other way around."

"What do you mean?"

She took his bony hand in hers. "You know, we've been together twenty years and we've never once talked about your origin story."

"It's not that complicated," Death Skull said. "I fell into a vat of toxic waste and it transformed me into an anthropomorphic skeleton."

"No, your *real* origin story," she said. "Middle school."

Death Skull grew even paler than usual as he recalled his years of being bullied. The names, the jokes, the pranks. By ninth grade it had gotten to the point where he was, like, "Maybe I *am* gay"—that's how much they'd gotten in his head. By the time he reached adulthood, he'd given up on trying to befriend people. It was safer to try to impress them, or if that failed, to knock them out with brightly colored gas. Being a monster hadn't made him lonely. Being lonely had made him a monster.

A loud peal of laughter pulled him from his reverie.

"It sounds like *The Bachelor*'s starting," he observed.

Jackie squeezed his knobby fingers. "Do you want to watch with us?"

The offer was tempting, but Death Skull managed to resist.

"Thank you," he said, rising to his feet. "But I've got work to do."

★ ★ ★

Death Skull sat at his supercomputer, plotting his next move. Fast Friends had refused to provide him with Doug's contact information on the grounds that they had not technically matched. That meant he had no choice but to resort to more nefarious means. He pulled up the website for the phone company and dialed up the helpline.

"This is Doug from Empire Mobile. Thank you for calling customer service. Your call may be recorded to ensure quality."

"Recorded?" Death Skull raised a craggy eyebrow, which was not visible to Doug. "Maybe we should tell them to mind their *phone* business?"

He laughed hysterically.

"Are you still there?" he asked after some time had passed.

"Yeah," Doug said.

"Listen, I'm sorry about before," he said.

"I'm not supposed to take personal calls," Doug said.

"What about making your own path? Living by your own rules?"

"I've gotta go."

"I just wanted to say that I've thought it over and I do want to hang out sometime."

"Well, I don't!" Doug said with a self-possession that caught Death Skull off guard. "I don't want to hang out with someone who's embarrassed to be seen with me."

"It's not like that," Death Skull said.

"I don't believe you," Doug said. "Thank you for calling Empire Mobile."

"Doug—!"

Death Skull grimaced as the phone went dead in his hands. But his disappointment gave way to resolve. He'd blown things with Doug—that much was certain—but that didn't mean he couldn't make things right.

He looked out the window and peered out at the city lights below. Yes, he could see it all now—a way to win back Doug's trust. The scheme was already forming in his mind, a plan so simple, it made him cackle hysterically.

I think I figured out how to work things out with Doug, he texted Jackie. *But you don't need to write back. I know you're watching the Bachelor. Enjoy the rest of the episode. We'll talk later. I love you.*

★ ★ ★

Death Skull sat in a ten-foot leather armchair, his black eyes reflecting the embers of his fireplace. Scuzz and Rumble stood on either side of him, their bulging arms folded in a show of menace.

"Ready boss?" Scuzz asked.

"Ready," Death Skull said.

He grinned as the camera flicked on, beaming his glowering face onto every TV screen in Empire City.

"This is Death Skull," he intoned. "And I've commandeered the airwaves. Don't try to change the channel. I'm the *bonely* show in town!"

Scuzz and Rumble fell on the ground, clutching their sides.

"Good one, boss!" Scuzz said.

"Yeah!" Rumble said. "Wowie zowie wow!"

Death Skull sighed. "Guys, come on," he said. "It wasn't that good."

"We thought it was!" Scuzz said, a panicked expression in his eyes.

"Yeah!" Rumble said.

"Okay," Death Skull said, letting the matter drop. He stared at the camera's blinking red light. There were millions of people watching him right now: Ultra Man, Mayor Price, probably some people that he went to high school with. But that was the whole point. He took a deep breath and kept going.

"I want to send a message to the people of Empire City," he said. "Normally, when I do this, it's to announce a crime that I'm planning to commit, which, as I'm saying it out loud, is a shortsighted thing for me to do. In any case, I recently signed up for a male friendship speed dating event because I've been having trouble making friends."

Scuzz and Rumble exchanged a look, which Death Skull clocked but ignored.

"While I was there," Death Skull said, "I met someone I thought was cool. His name is Doug and he works for the phone company. And I know he's watching, because we're three minutes into the new episode of *Rick and Morty*. Doug, I want you to know that I've finally watched some episodes online, and you were right. I love the show. It's so good. And this episode I've interrupted is going to be on *again* tomorrow night, and I've decided to host a watch party in my apartment. So, no pressure whatsoever, but if you're not still mad at me, I'd love it if you could make it. I know I didn't make the greatest first impression. I've got a lot of work to do on myself. But I'm not a bad guy, or at least I don't want to be a bad guy anymore. And I know that normally I end these things by doing that crazy laughing thing, where the camera pushes in on my face while I just absolutely lose it, but this time I'm just going to put up my cell phone number, and, Doug, you can text if you want, but again, no pressure. That's it. That's everything. Good night."

He turned to his henchmen as the camera flickered off.

"You guys are invited, too," he said. "But it's seriously optional. If you're too busy, I won't be offended, or choke you out or anything like that. That's not who I am anymore."

Scuzz and Rumble exchanged a hopeful look.

"Does that mean you'll transform us back into humans?" Scuzz asked.

"Well, no, I can't do that," Death Skull said. "That's not how toxic waste works."

"So these changes to our bodies are permanent."

"Yeah."

"So I'm always going to be, like, this rhinoceros."

"Yeah."

"Man," Scuzz said. "Fuck."

Death Skull flashed him a playful smirk. "At least you can say you're really a *made man!*"

He paused for laughter, but Scuzz just stared in silence at his hooves.

"I can't believe I'm going to die like this," he said.

"I'm really sorry," Death Skull said. "How about I pay for plastic surgery? There's got to be a way to at least shave down the hooves into the shape of feet. That's something, right?"

"It's better than nothing," Scuzz acknowledged.

Death Skull's phone buzzed, and he frantically pulled it from his robe. He'd told himself it didn't matter whether Doug agreed to his terms—that he'd already done something valuable simply by reaching out. But when the text came in, it felt like a diamond in his hand.

★ ★ ★

"Do I put the limes in whole?" Death Skull asked.

"No," Jackie said. "You just want to put in the juice."

"Oh," Death Skull said.

"Don't worry," Jackie said. "You're going to do great." She checked her watch. "I better get going. Marlyse made a reservation."

Death Skull watched as she checked her lipstick in the mirror. "Look at us," he said. "You're seeing friends, and I'm seeing friends." He hesitated. "We're not so different, you and I."

She pulled him in for a kiss. There was a knock on the door, and Jackie was about to say something reassuring, but Death Skull was already bounding down the hallway, his bony fingers trembling with excitement. He took three deep breaths to steady himself and swung open the door. Doug was wearing the same shirt as last time, but at some point, he'd managed to remove the fasteners.

"Hey," he said.

"Hey," said Death Skull.

He wasn't sure whether to shake Doug's hand or hug him, so he split the difference, pumping his fist with one hand while sort of rubbing his shoulder with the other.

"This is Scuzz and Rumble," he said, leading Doug into the living room. "They haven't seen *Rick and Morty* yet."

"You're gonna love it," Doug told them. "Oh, I brought Fritos, by the way."

"Thanks," Death Skull said, taking the bag. "Hopefully you'll get more than half a chip this time!"

Doug and Death Skull shared a gentle chuckle.

"I don't get it," Scuzz admitted.

"It's an inside joke we have," said Death Skull proudly. "But don't worry. I'll tell you all about it."

KEROSENE

Kerosene was a miracle invention. Powerful, odorless, and cheap, it made whale oil obsolete. And Rufus Vanderhoot had ridden the wave right to the top. In the five years since opening his refinery, he'd become the richest man in Boston. There were Shetland ponies for the children, Parisian hats for the wife, and Bolivian cocaine for Rufus. His favorite purchase, though, was his pleasure yacht, a ninety-foot beauty that he sailed daily, circling the harbor in a kind of never-ending victory lap. And that's what he was doing along with cocaine one Sunday morning when he heard a feeble cry in the distance.

Rufus raised his bejeweled spyglass and gasped at the sight of the wreck drifting his way. Its deck was empty, except for an emaciated man with wild eyes and a filthy, tangled beard. He wore a captain's hat but was otherwise completely naked.

"Ho!" Rufus shouted.

His crew stared at him with confusion. "Ho" was not a sailing term, and Rufus had just blurted it out at random because he had no nautical knowledge.

"Shall we pick him up, sir?" asked one of his servants helpfully.

"Yes," Rufus said.

He held on tight as his crew sped toward the battered ship and secured a towline around what remained of its mast. The captain was too weak to walk, so they had to transport him to the yacht on one of Rufus's chaise longues. The old man's voice was raspy from disuse, but after some frantic swigs of broth, he managed to croak out a question.

"What year is it?"

Rufus handed him a newspaper and the captain let out a startled scream.

"Arr," he said. "It's been ten years."

Rufus shook his head in disbelief. "My God," he said. "How did you survive?"

"Just straight-up cannibalism," replied the captain. "Eating me beloved brothers, one by one."

"You poor soul," Rufus said. "It sounds like you've been through hell."

"Aye," said the captain. "But at least all me suffering be worth it." He pointed at his battered ship with one of his few remaining fingers. "That hull be full of oil. And not just any oil. *Whale* oil. The finest fuel known to mankind!" He grinned at the kerosene mogul. "Aye, whenever I wake up screaming from a nightmare, I just remind meself that all the hardships I faced be absolutely necessary."

Rufus said nothing. His crew, he noticed, had at some point slipped below deck, leaving him alone with the captain.

"Arr, I feel like I've been monopolizing the conversation," said the captain. "Tell me about yourself. What is it you be doing for a living?"

"Oh, this and that," Rufus said evasively.

"You must be successful," said the captain. "No man meat on the table. On my ship, we had to eat each other!"

"You mentioned that," Rufus said.

"Arr, forgive me," said the captain. "My memory hasn't been the same since a whale headbutted me brain." He squinted toward shore; day had turned to night, and the lamplighters were busily firing up the kerosene lanterns that dotted every street.

"Boston seems *brighter* than I remember it," observed the captain, his bushy white brows scrunched in thought. "People must be using more whale oil than ever!" He flashed Rufus another grin. "That's good for me! Given I be selling whale oil."

"Uh-huh," Rufus said noncommittally.

"I had to kill me best friend to eat his heart," the captain volunteered. "He begged me to do it, but that didn't make it any easier. Even the whales knew that it be wrong. They kept shaking their heads back and forth, like, 'Stop. This be crazy.'" He chuckled. "All worth it, of course."

They were nearly to shore now. For the first time since becoming rich, Rufus felt a bead of sweat slide down his forehead.

"Say, captain," he said. "Why don't I buy your whale oil? That way you don't have to come to shore at all. You can just sail on to Tahiti, ideally without talking to anyone, or looking at anything."

"Arr, that be very generous of you," the captain said. "But I should really be testing my whale oil's value on the open market. Something tells me I'm in for a pleasant surprise!" He sniffed the air. "That's odd," he said, eyeing the swiftly nearing streetlights. "Those whale oil lamps don't seem to smell very strongly of whale." He furrowed his brow again. "Wait a minute..."

Rufus averted his eyes as the captain leapt to his feet and pointed an accusatory finger at him. "Did they *invent* something while I was gone?"

"I'm afraid so," Rufus admitted.

The captain let out a rueful sigh. "I always knew this day would come," he said. "The day when scientists would invent a new kind of whale oil lamp that would stop the whale oil from smelling bad, thereby increasing the popularity of whale oil. And now that it's happened, I can't help but dance a happy jig! Whale oil's my line, you see."

"I'm aware," Rufus said, rubbing his throbbing temples.

"Aye, forgive me," said the captain. "Sometimes when I get going about whale oil, it be hard to stop, because it be so central to me life. I've got no family, no friends, no hobbies. I'm not even into sports. You know what I be doing for fun, at night? I be reading books about how to improve me whale oil business." He furrowed his brow again. "It's funny. I haven't been seeing many new releases in that category lately." He shrugged. "Well, I'm sure there will be more soon, given whale oil's enduring popularity!"

Rufus snorted some cocaine. "Okay, look," he said. "There's something I've got to tell you. While you were at sea eating your friends, scientists invented a new fuel called kerosene. And it's—"

"Inferior to whale oil?"

Rufus looked the captain in the eye.

"It's better. I've made millions selling it. And I can assure you that no one, anywhere, will ever buy whale oil again."

"Arr," said the captain.

The men sat in silence for a minute, the waves lapping softly at the hull.

"I don't 'love' this," said the captain.

"I'm truly sorry," Rufus said, placing a hand on the captain's sun-scorched shoulder.

"It's not your fault," the captain said. "It's like they say: 'Sometimes, you end up on the wrong side of the harpoon.'"

"They don't say that anymore."

"Arr."

The captain stood up and cracked his neck.

"Well, I suppose I should be on me way."

Rufus watched with confusion as the captain threw a rope around his waist and began to lower himself into the frothy waves.

"Where are you going?"

"Back to me boat," he said. "If there be no one buying whale oil, there be no reason for me to waste a night in boring, racist Boston."

"Where will you go instead?" Rufus demanded.

"Where else?" said the captain. "Back to sea, to hunt more whales!"

"You must not have heard me," Rufus said. "The entire whaling industry is —"

"Obsolete, yes, I know. But I never whaled for the money. I did it for the love of the chase, the cool, salty breeze in me hair, the thrill of the wheel in me hand, the sense, however foolish, that I be in charge of me own destiny."

"You described it as a living hell."

"Aye, complaining be one of the things I love the most about it. People are impressed, and also, it be giving me an excuse to drink."

"But how will you survive?" Rufus pressed. "Even if you catch more whales, nobody will want to buy the oil."

"I'm independently wealthy."

Rufus was taken aback. "Really?"

"Aye," said the captain. "Me dad, he be inventing a medical instrument. You've never heard of it, but it's become the standard of care for all gallbladder procedures, and whenever it's used, I be getting a royalty."

"Wow," Rufus said. "Is it a lot?"

"Arr, no," the captain said. "I'm not rich or anything. But so what? They've done studies and there be no correlation between money and happiness!" He paused. "I mean, you have to be above a certain threshold, obviously."

"Right."

"Like the thing I be reading, it be saying that up to seventy-five K it be mattering a lot how much you make, because if you be making less than that, you be stressed out all the time. But once you be making seventy-five K, beyond that, it all be more or less the same."

"So you make more than seventy-five K a year from medical royalties?"

"Aye."

"How much?"

"Arr, I don't feel comfortable saying the exact amount. But it be enough so that I be comfortable."

"A hundred and fifty? *Two hundred?*"

"Arr, I'd prefer not to say."

"Six figures, though?"

"Aye, but let's be moving off it now because I be getting uncomfortable."

"Just tell me," Rufus said.

"Arr, no, I don't be feeling comfortable."

And with that he cut his rope line free and splashed his way across the moonlit waves. Rufus rolled his eyes as the captain crawled aboard his wreck and broke into a wild, carefree shanty. The old coot was obviously deluding himself. A man needed more than salty breezes. He needed a purpose, a sense that his life was worthwhile. Whaling was worse than futile: it was immoral. Lives would be lost, and nature despoiled, for a cause that future generations would look at as barbaric and unnecessary. It was horrible to contemplate. He lowered his spyglass and turned with relief to the shore, where his factory awaited him, and the black smoke billowed as high as he could see.

GOLIATH

Goliath looked down at the familiar crowd of reporters. He'd participated in so many press conferences he doubted they had anything left to ask him. Everyone already knew his height (four cubits), his record (undefeated), and even his favorite prefight meal (meats). Still, the journalists looked as eager to talk to him as ever. The etchers were jostling for position and the reporters were vigorously wiping down their slates to make room for his sound bites. Goliath couldn't help but feel a tiny surge of pride. He'd been fighting people to the death for years, and somehow everybody was still interested.

A reporter threw up his hand and Goliath dutifully called on him.

"You have question for Goliath?"

"Yes, thank you!" the reporter said, shouting to make himself heard over the hubbub. "What are your thoughts on fighting David?"

Goliath scratched his beard. He wasn't sure who David was. In the early days of his career, he'd always made sure to research his opponents, taking note of their strengths and weaknesses. But he'd stopped after figuring out he could reliably beat anyone simply by ripping out their spine.

"Who is David?" he asked.

As if on cue, a small blond boy walked across the dais, his floppy hair bouncing with each stride. He sat in the chair next to Goliath's and squinted up at his microphone, which was positioned several feet above his head.

"Uh...little help?" he said, flashing the press an endearing grin.

The reporters laughed with delight as an officiant lowered the microphone to David's level.

"Wow, this is so cool!" David said. "I can't believe I'm at a real-life press conference! I hope I don't mess up!" He paused to let an "Aww" finish rippling through the crowd. "So how does this even *work*? Do I call on people *myself*? Wow! Okay, I guess I'll start with...Shana."

"Thank you, David," said a well-dressed reporter in the front row, who Goliath didn't recognize. "I guess the question we all want to know is, what makes you believe that a small, poor, unarmed child can defeat a well-known giant in a death match?"

"Honestly," David said, "I'm just grateful for the opportunity to fight at all. Growing up small, poor, and unarmed, I never imagined I'd ever get the chance to do anything noteworthy. It's all thanks to my mom. Being a single mother is no joke. If you ask me, she's the *real* underdog death fighter."

Goliath watched in bafflement as the reporters all scribbled down the quote. It had not been about fighting, and yet for some reason they had found it newsworthy.

"Let's get someone in the back," David said. "How about you, sexy?"

An older man stood up, blushing. "Thank you, David," he said, looking a bit flustered. "My question is about determination. Do you have it?"

"Great question," David said. "Yes."

The reporters burst into applause.

"That was two in a row for David," Goliath noted. "Usually, it goes back and forth. One question for Goliath, one for other death fighter, then Goliath speak again."

The room fell silent.

"Okay, I've got one," someone said eventually. "How impressed are you by David?"

"Goliath confused," the giant admitted. "David is boy. Goliath is giant. We should not even be fighting.

Goliath do not understand what is happening. Goliath confused."

The reporters gave a low, collective murmur.

"David," Shana said solemnly. "How would you respond to Goliath's hurtful statement?"

David remained silent for a beat, apparently weighing his words carefully.

"There's always going to be ignorance," he said. "That's just the world we live in. I mean, shit, I've been dealing with naysayers since the jump. People saying, 'D's too poor, D's too small, D's too unarmed.' Skeebo knows what I'm talking about."

A man in a leather vest who Goliath guessed was Skeebo flashed David a thumbs-up.

"There's always going to be people who can't see the vision," David continued. "And maybe I shouldn't be saying this, but the truth is, I *like* those people. Because they're the ones who keep me motivated. When I'm up at four a.m. doing crunches with Mateo, and someone's like, 'Hey, did you see who just called you unarmed?,' or 'a small child,' or whatever, that shit's my *fuel*. I fucking live for that shit."

Goliath felt his stomach rumble. He hadn't eaten meat in over fifteen minutes. He hoped David would stop talking soon so he could eat some meat.

"Because the thing you gotta know by now," David

was saying, "is I ain't doing this shit for me. I'm doing it for all those kids in Bethlehem who get told every day of their lives, 'You'll never get to be a death fighter.' Like, you all know how much I hate to talk about my charity shit, because that's not why I do it, but there's a *reason* why I'm back in the hood every Hanukkah, handing out briskets: because I'm fighting for Bethlehem, and D's always gonna rep the Beth, straight up."

The reporters all nodded emphatically.

"So, if you ask me what I think about Goliath's comments?" David said. "Here's all I'll say. D's gonna be D. What you see is what you get. No fronting, no filter. Just some kid from the Beth, trying to shine his ass off. That's who I am. That's D."

"Goliath hungry," Goliath said. "Can Goliath go?" There didn't seem to be anyone paying attention to him. "Okay," Goliath said, standing up. "Goliath go."

Goliath ate a full-size pig and burped contentedly. It had been a long, strange day, but now he was at peace, sitting across from his twelve-year-old daughter, Jules. Sundays were their night together and by far the highlight of his week.

"How is pig?" Goliath asked.

"Fine," Jules said.

"There is dessert, too," Goliath said. "Other pig."

"Okay," Jules said.

Goliath studied his daughter's inscrutable expression. She had inherited his shyness, along with his size and hairiness, and it wasn't easy to get her to open up. Middle school so far had not been easy. The other kids made fun of her for the tiniest of things: her height, her width, the depth of her voice, the fullness of her unibrow, the crash of her steps, the heat of her breath, the unsettlingly audible sound of her eyeblinks. Add dyslexia to the mix and private school had seemed like the only option. But two months into the school year, Goliath still had no idea if the transfer had paid off. He didn't care about the academic side of things (even the private schools in Philistine weren't particularly good), but he was determined to help his daughter recapture her spark, the light that her peers seemed to have stolen from her.

"How is Northridge Academy?" Goliath asked. "You tell Goliath how it is going at Northridge Academy."

"Fine," Jules said.

"Are there bullies like last school?" Goliath pressed.

"No," Jules said.

Goliath placed his giant hand on hers and continued in a gentle tone. "If there are bullies, you can tell Goliath. Goliath will kill them."

"There aren't any bullies," she said, pulling her hand away.

"Okay," Goliath said. "Goliath drop it."

Jules picked absently at her pig.

"The best way is to tear along the sockets," Goliath said. "Goliath help?"

"That's okay," she said. "I need to do my algebra."

Goliath sighed as she trudged off to her bedroom, stooping to avoid hitting the ceiling. He could still remember how she used to laugh as a baby when he threw her in the air — a giddy high-pitched giggle, followed by several seconds of silence as she experienced free fall, then a happy sigh as she landed in his arms. Back then, it had been so easy to give her what she needed.

She was trying to squeeze through her doorframe when Goliath noticed something protruding from her backpack: a brightly colored flyer.

"What is flyer?" he asked.

"Nothing," Jules said. "Just something from theater club."

Goliath leapt to his full four-cubit height. "You joined *club*?"

"It's no big deal," Jules said.

"No big deal?" Goliath roared. "It is *huge* deal!"

"I just signed up because my friends did."

"Friends? What friends?"

Jules blushed, aware that she'd revealed more than she'd intended.

"Who are friends?" Goliath demanded. "You tell Goliath! You give friends' names, and say how you met, and describe everybody's deal!"

Jules wrenched the doorframe wider with her hands and muscled her way into her room. Still, Goliath was ecstatic. All at once, he could envision a sparkling future for Jules, full of parties and laughter and all kinds of victories. He was triumphantly tearing into his dessert pig when she poked her head out through her mangled doorway.

"Oh, and Mom says you need to call the school," she said. "Something about tuition."

Goliath blinked loudly as her door slammed in his face.

Goliath had never been great at managing his finances. Whenever he tried to keep track of his expenses, he would get confused and then lose consciousness. But he knew enough to realize that he was in serious trouble. Gretchen had gotten almost everything in the divorce. His death fights paid decently, and there were some incentives built into his contract, like if he won in the first round or ripped somebody's dick off. But even if he managed both with David, he still wouldn't be able to cover Jules's tuition. His only hope was to find an additional source of income. Luckily, he knew just where to start.

"Goliath never do endorsement before," he told Skeebo, as he took a seat in the manager's palatial office.

"Neither had David when he met me," Skeebo said. "Now the kid's so hot everyone's creaming themselves to get a fucking piece. Signature sandal, signature tunic. They took a drop of sweat from his balls to make a fragrance and it sold out in a day. Kid's got a production company, D Street, started as a vanity label for his raps, now the Saudis want to invest. And all that shit—*all that shit*—is *nothing* compared to the meet and greets." He looked over his shoulder, then continued in a low, intense voice. "That meet and greet shit is something you would not believe. These people, they come on their camels and they wait in the desert heat for hours. And the kid walks down the line with his guys, doesn't shake anyone's hand, 'cause he's a germophobe, just kind of gives a little wave, and everyone just starts straight-up weeping. And we charge them twenty silver pieces just to stand there, plus fifty for a commemorative scroll. And it's a million degrees out and we make them pay us for the water. The *water*! When we started doing that shit, even I was like, 'This might be too far.

Like, this is some kind of *human rights* shit.' But these people don't think twice about it. They buy four, five, six waters apiece. I'm telling you, this meet and greet thing, it's fucked up."

Goliath nodded. Skeebo had been talking a long time.

"So anyway," Skeebo said. "Let's get into it."

Goliath watched hopefully as Skeebo whipped out his slate.

"Okay, so I asked around town, put out a bunch of feelers with all kinds of brands."

"How did brands respond to Goliath?"

"We didn't have much luck with luxury, lifestyle, or apparel," Skeebo said. "But we did get an offer from Red Light. It's a good offer, very fair for what they're asking. That's the good news."

"What is bad news?"

"It's not necessarily bad news," Skeebo said. "It's just some more context for you to have as you weigh your decision. This company, Red Light...are you at all familiar with them?"

"No."

"Okay," Skeebo said. "Well, just so you're going into this with eyes wide open, Red Light happens to be a pornographic company."

"They want Goliath to have sex with someone?"

"No, of course not!" Skeebo said. "Nothing like that. There's not even any nudity, beyond the kind of thing that you would normally wear during your fights. But it would still be in the pornographic category."

"Goliath do not understand."

"Just the way it would be produced, released, and marketed; it would not be considered mainstream work. Red Light is great, by the way. I've done deals with them before, and they're totally reputable, no mob stuff, like, if you're going to do porn, they're, like, the gold standard for porn. But they are a porn company, and this is a porn offer, and I'm not going to sit across from you and say, 'This isn't porn,' because it's porn."

"Goliath do not want to do porn."

"Okay, cool!" Skeebo said. "See, that's why we do this, just to get the lay of the land."

"Please move on to next offer," Goliath said.

"Unfortunately, there are no other offers."

Goliath shook his head in disbelief. "Why not?"

"The brands all want David. Do you realize he's gotten so popular that people are naming their *kids* after him? No joke. 'David' is becoming, like, a normal, common name that regular people have."

"Why don't people like Goliath? Goliath has been winning for years."

"That's the problem," Skeebo said. "Have you heard the saying 'Nobody roots for Goliath'?"

"No."

"It's new. The point is that audiences just don't find you appealing. They see David as way more authentic, root-able, and likable."

Goliath growled in frustration. He understood why people sympathized with David. He was small and about to be murdered. But it's not like Goliath had it easy. If the public knew the pressure he was under, then surely their allegiances would change.

"Goliath will get more endorsements," he vowed. "Goliath just need to show people real Goliath."

"So yes to Red Light?"

"No!" Goliath thundered, his eyes narrowing with determination. "Goliath have smarter idea."

★ ★ ★

Goliath sat across from Shana on a small wooden stage in the desert. Although her talk show was new, it had become extremely popular thanks to her celebrity interviews, which so far had all been with David. Now it was Goliath's turn in the hot seat, and there were thousands assembled to see how he would manage.

He shifted uncomfortably in his tiny chair, thinking about Jules. She still had no idea she might have to leave

Northridge Academy. Goliath told himself it was because he didn't want to stress her out before her first big improv show, but deep down he knew he was protecting his own ego. Jules was getting older, but she still saw him as strong, indomitable—a giant. He couldn't bear to let her down.

Jules hadn't yet told him the names or the deals of any of her friends from theater club. But their influence was obvious to him. Until recently, she'd always worn her hair the same way: in a tangled, unwashed clump that covered her entire face and body. Lately, though, she'd begun to tie it back with a system of ropes, and the smile it revealed was a revelation: confident, composed, content. It was this smile he pictured as Shana introduced him to the crowd.

"My next guest is an undefeated death fighter who has represented Philistine for years. His next match will be against David, who represents everybody here as well as the one true God. Goliath, thanks for being with us."

"Thank you for having Goliath," said the giant, smiling through the crowd's tepid applause.

"I understand there's something you would like to clear up."

"Yes, thank you," Goliath said, clearing his throat. "People think Goliath have it easy. But really Goliath have things hard."

"Say more," Shana said.

Goliath turned toward the crowd, a mix of peasants, slaves, and lepers.

"When Goliath was young," he began, "Goliath so big that Goliath had to eat more food than other kids, and it would take long time. Sometimes Goliath would have to sit at table twenty minutes longer than everybody else. So there is that. Also, it is not easy killing people. Sometimes, blood splashes onto Goliath's clothes and it is wet. And number three: it is hard for Goliath to buy pants. In conclusion: Goliath history's greatest victim."

The crowd began to boo. Goliath could sense he wasn't off to a great start. He reached for a nearby mug of water, but to him it was the equivalent of a thimble, and the liquid failed to even coat his tongue.

"Forgive me for being skeptical," Shana said. "Because when I look at you, I don't see hardship. What I see, frankly, is a lot of privilege."

"Let Goliath explain better," he said as sweat poured down his muscled back. "People think Goliath is rich, but Goliath is not rich. Goliath merely comfortable. There is difference between rich and comfortable!"

The boos grew louder.

"Please!" Goliath begged. "You do not understand what you are doing! If you do not start worshipping

Goliath, Goliath will not score cushy endorsement deals, and he will not even be able to send daughter to private school! He will have to send her to public school with poor people! People as poor as you!"

Goliath shielded his face as the audience pelted him with sand. By the time he recovered his vision, the show was over, the crowd was gone, and Skeebo was standing beside him, looking contrite.

"Hey G, I'm sorry," he said. "But that porn offer went away."

"Goliath understand," said the giant. And for a change, he meant it.

★ ★ ★

Goliath sat across from Jules, their uneaten pigs between them. He'd offered to host a party for her Northridge friends, so she could say goodbye, but she had turned him down.

"At least you do not have to wear uniform anymore!" Goliath said. "That is one good thing!"

"Uh-huh," Jules said. Her voice was muted by the tangle of hair that once again shielded her from view.

"Maybe you can start theater club at public school?" Goliath suggested.

Jules said nothing.

"That is what you will do," Goliath said. "You will

tell public school you want to start theater club. And you will start it, and do improv at assemblies, and before you know it, you will become star."

"I don't want to be a star," Jules said. "That's not why I like theater."

Goliath leaned forward. This was the most Jules had confided in him in several years and he was determined not to lose the thread.

"Why do you like theater?" he asked.

Jules looked up from her plate, and through her curtain of hair, Goliath could glimpse her teary eyes.

"Because you get to be somebody else," she said.

Goliath winced like he'd been struck by more sand. He wanted to tell her she was wrong—that she could still become anything she wanted. But she was too old to fall for such a blatant lie. The truth was that other people decided who you were, and once they did you could never change their minds. It was like trying to rip apart a pig. You could strain and pull in any direction you wanted, but your only real hope was to tear along the sockets, to accept what had been heaped onto your plate.

He yanked off a haunch and slowly chewed.

★ ★ ★

Goliath flexed as the audience bombarded him with trash.

"Goliath have message for haters!" he roared. "Your beloved David is about to die! And not in a normal way! Think of craziest way you can think of! It will be crazier than that!"

Goliath rarely spoke before his fights, preferring to let his killing do the talking, but this time he'd screamed himself hoarse. And by the time he climbed into the ring, it was obvious his taunts had made an impact. David's normally buoyant blond bob lay flat on his head, matted down by sweat, and his bright blue eyes looked bloodshot.

"Yo, bruh, check it out," he said, flashing the giant a smile. "That dis verse that came out, I didn't mean nothing by it. When I did it in the studio, I didn't even know they were recording. And next thing I know, my boys call me up and they're like, 'Dog, it's a bop, it's on the album,' and I'm like, 'For real?' You know how it is."

"Goliath kill you soon," the giant said.

David swallowed as the referee launched into his usual prefight remarks.

"Okay, you fellows know the rules. Everything's allowed. Just go crazy. Kill each other."

Goliath nodded as the referee climbed out of the ring and went home.

David looked even smaller than usual in his fight outfit, a glossy loincloth embossed with D Street Productions' graffiti-inspired logo.

"Yo Skeebo," he called out to his manager. "Maybe we should postpone this bitch?"

"It's too late," Skeebo said matter-of-factly. "But I'll see you after at the meet and greet."

"Fuck," David said.

Goliath cracked his neck and stretched his killing muscles. The crowd was chanting David's name, but in the ring, the sound was barely audible. All he could hear was David's frantic breathing and his own thudding footsteps as he walked toward his opponent, engulfing the boy with his shadow.

Goliath smirked as David fumbled for his slingshot, his signature model, the D1. It had been designed with consumers in mind and was far too small for use in professional combat. It wobbled in his hands as he slid in a pebble and feebly drew it back. The crowd fell silent; they knew this shot would be David's one chance. If he failed to connect, his spine would be within the giant's reach. Goliath could hear a few hushed prayers as David aimed his pebble heavenward and limply let it fly.

Goliath watched as the small stone drifted toward him in a long, slow arc. He thought about the trophies he had won, the belts he had hoisted, the dicks he'd ripped off. He thought about the way it felt to win a fight, the unmatchable clarity that could come only with victory, that sense, however fleeting, that you had been born for a reason. So far, his fights had all been easy. This one would be hard.

The pebble was drifting off course, blown wide by a gentle desert breeze. Goliath took a deep breath and lunged into its path.

"Ow!" he shouted as the pebble bounced harmlessly off his muscled brow. "Goliath lose death fight!" He lay on the ground and closed his eyes. "David beat Goliath."

He knew it wasn't the kind of performance that would have passed muster in theater club, but the crowd seemed to buy it, screaming and crying in ecstasy. Amazingly, David bought it, too. "Yeah, bruh!" he shouted as his entourage carried him away. "All day!"

Goliath kept his eyes closed until the cheering faded into silence. When he finally opened them, Skeebo was smiling down at him, holding a sack of silver pieces. Their deal had been simple. In exchange for the dive, Goliath would receive an anonymous stake in D Street Productions going forward. As long as David's star continued to rise — and it assuredly would after this upset — Goliath could cover Jules's tuition indefinitely. He was gleefully reaching for his payment when Skeebo yanked it out of reach.

"Hold up," he said, his smile fading. "You still gotta sign an NDA."

"What is NDA?" Goliath asked.

Skeebo looked over his shoulder and continued in an ominous whisper. "It means you can never tell anyone what happened here. Not the public, not the press, not David. Not even your own family."

For the first time, Goliath pondered the full scope of what he had agreed to. Something told him that this battle was the kind of thing people might remember. It was possible the public would even embellish his loss over the years, saying he'd died in the fight, or that David had cut off his head. Even Jules would grow up thinking he'd been beaten. His legacy of greatness would end, and instead, he would become a reference point for failure, an eternal symbol of humiliation, and all so his daughter could stay in a club where you stood in a circle, clapping your hands and saying, "Zip, zap, zop."

He signed the slate and grabbed the cash, feeling gigantic.

IV

THANKSGIVING RIDER

This document acknowledges that Lauren ("Talent") has agreed to appear for a MAXIMUM of THREE (3) days and TWO (2) nights at the residence of her mother ("Venue") during the Thanksgiving holiday, pursuant to the terms of this agreement.

Accommodations

Venue will provide Talent with complete, private access to her childhood bedroom (aka "the Pilates room") for the duration of her appearance. It is additionally agreed that, during Talent's visit, Venue's new husband ("VNH") will abstain completely from the use of Talent's bathroom. Venue is responsible for communicating this deal point to VNH and monitoring him daily after breakfast to ensure this stipulation is enforced. Furthermore, if this agreement is broken, and VNH uses

Talent's bathroom, Venue will not tell Talent that it's "no big deal," or laugh when VNH makes his usual joke to Talent about air fresheners. Venue is aware that Talent's bathroom has no ventilation, and is located right next to Talent's bed, and that by using Talent's bathroom, VNH is effectively going to the bathroom in her bed. Venue understands that VNH's use of Talent's bathroom is a major violation of her space and so disrespectful that it is basically on par with assault. Venue will not gaslight Talent into thinking she is crazy for being furious that VNH has used her bathroom.

Cancellation Policy

Honestly, if VNH uses Talent's bathroom, Talent will just fly back to San Francisco. She will literally just walk right out the house without saying goodbye to anyone and take an Uber to the airport and that will be that. There are THREE (3) other bathrooms in the house, just tell VNH to use one of the MANY OTHER BATHROOMS.

Alcohol

Venue shall provide Talent with unlimited, unmonitored access to a fully stocked bar for the duration of her appearance, featuring a MINIMUM of:

a) ONE (1) gallon-size handle of vodka
b) An adequate supply of orange juice, Diet Coke, and other mixers to enable Talent to consume vodka discreetly
c) FIVE (5) bottles of drinkable white wine
d) Sundry beers

Venue will not comment on the quantity of Talent's drinking during her appearance, or monitor "level" of vodka in bottle. Talent will be drinking and that's just going to be what it is. Talent will also go outside sometimes to smoke weed, and that's not going to be a thing either, that's just going to be treated as a normal thing.

Recent Layoff

Talent will perform ONE (1) five-minute summary of her recent layoff from her start-up, including a GENERAL description of what the start-up did, and a BRIEF explanation for its failure. Talent will not answer questions about current state of finances, health insurance status, or job prospects.

Venue agrees not to make reference to the article she read entitled "Top Ten High-Paying Jobs That Literally Anyone Can Do with Zero Experience." Venue understands that she has already emailed and texted article to Talent THREE (3) times. Venue is additionally aware that said article is not a real article, but a click-bait advertisement generated by CareerMonkey.com, designed to trick people into buying a subscription to that site. Venue will not debate this fact by pointing at article's "byline," as "proof" that it's a "real article." Venue will accept the reality that many online ads are given bylines now, in order to make them look like real articles. If Venue insists "This one looks real," Talent will zoom in on the "article," show Venue where it says "Paid Post," and the debate will be settled. Venue will not read the words "Paid Post" out loud, in a suspicious tone of voice, and then shrug at VNH in a way that implies that there is still some ambiguity left about whether it is a real article. Venue will just admit, for once in her life, that she was wrong about one thing. Jesus.

Transportation

Venue agrees to reimburse Talent $432 for the cost of her round-trip plane ticket, but will not tell anyone that she had to do that, especially not Talent's Perfect Doctor Brother with His Perfect Wife and Perfect Children (TPDBHPWPC).

Klonopin

On the night before TPDBHPWPC arrives, Talent will take Klonopin.

Lighting Requirements

The following morning (aka "Thanksgiving"), Venue will refrain from entering Talent's bedroom and opening Talent's blinds in a passive-aggressive attempt to wake her up. If Venue breaks this stipulation, she will ADMIT her intention was to wake up Talent. Venue will not make up insane lie about wanting "to let air in." Venue is aware that opening blinds does not let air in. Opening WINDOWS lets air in. Opening blinds just lets in bright, punishing light, right into Talent's face.

Rehearsal Time

When TPDBHPWPC pulls in with his station wagon, Talent requires FIVE (5) minutes to drink some coffee and just mentally prepare for all those fucking kids and all the questions about her getting fired and the goddam dance with her perfect sister-in-law Jenn about who's going to do the stupid pie.

Meet and Greet

After drinking a MINIMUM of TWO (2) cups of coffee, Talent agrees to participate in a meet and greet session with TPDBHPWPC's latest perfect baby and pose for a MAXIMUM of THREE (3) photographs holding said baby.

Cancellation Policy

If VNH makes ANY kind of comment implying that Talent should have a baby by this point in her life, even if it is said in the most lighthearted, innocuous way (e.g., "You look pretty good holding one of those!"), it is Uber, airport, tearing through the sky to SF. What fucking right does VNH have to say shit? He has been in the picture for a MAXIMUM of FOUR (4) years (unless he and Venue met while Dad was STILL ALIVE, which is math we'll get into if this kind of shit keeps happening).

Thanksgiving Meal Requirements

Talent shall be seated as far as possible from VNH, on the "wine side" of the table. Talent will not be required to initiate conversation during meal. Talent agrees to politely listen to a MAXIMUM of TWO (2) dry updates about her high school classmates' parents who still live in town, provided they are of reasonable length and do not contain digressions about local real estate developments. Talent will not point out each time Venue repeats a story but will internally keep track of the repetitions.

In between dinner and dessert, Talent will corner TPDBHPWPC in the kitchen and ask him his medical opinion about Venue's fading memory. Talent will be startled to hear from TPDBHPWPC that Venue's senility is "age appropriate." When Talent pushes back, TPDBHPWPC will tell Talent that Venue's mental deterioration would be less of a shock if she had observed it more gradually, over the course of several visits, the implication being that she should visit Venue more. Talent will remind TPDBHPWPC that she works in San Francisco, and TPDBHPWPC will point out that she doesn't "work there anymore." Talent will be fucking devastated. Talent will catch sight of a faded family photo on the wall of a half-remembered trip to Sarasota, of Venue posing with Talent and TPDBHPWPC in some low-rent water park. Talent will try to mentally calculate Venue's age in the picture, but will be too drunk to do the math and will make TPDBHPWPC do it for her. Talent will be stunned to learn that Venue is TWO (2) years YOUNGER in the picture than Talent is now. Talent just won't be able to believe that. It will almost be too crazy to process. Talent will be rocked by the sense that she is hurtling toward death with nothing to show for her FORTY (40) years on the planet but wasted potential. TPDBHPWPC will tell Talent that he needs to get back into the living room because his 2-year-old is missing and probably making a mess. Talent will grip TPDBHPWPC's wrist and ask him if he thinks Dad was proud of her before he died, even though she never paid him back for her ill-conceived masters in museum studies. Talent will start to cry and not understand why she is crying. Jenn will come in to check on her pie and quickly back out of the room. TPDBHPWPC will reiterate to Talent that he needs to search for his missing 2-year-old. Talent will grip TPD-BHPWPC's wrist even harder and ask him if he thinks she's too old to apply to law school, or business school, and if he thinks she should get back together with Dane again, even though they had zero sexual connection. TPDBHPWPC will suggest that Talent drink ONE (1) glass of water.

When TPDBHPWPC is gone, Talent will stand alone in the dim kitchen for a MINIMUM of FIVE (5) minutes just completely spiraling, thinking about the darkest, most fucked-up shit. Talent will inwardly acknowledge that it was a mistake to use her loss of health insurance as an excuse to pause therapy.

Talent will feel a tug on her jeans. Talent will look down and see that TPDBHPWPC's Missing 2-Year-Old

(M2YO) has wandered into the kitchen at some point because he smelled pie. M2YO will ask Talent for pie. Talent will realize that M2YO probably doesn't know her name, or even how they're related, because they've only met a MAXIMUM of THREE (3) times, and she forgot to mail him a birthday present this year because she is a worthless piece of shit. Talent will tearfully tell him that she is his Aunt Lauren, and that she is sorry for forgetting his birthday, and M2YO will shrug with absolute indifference, because he has no conception of time or genetic relatedness, and he will ask again for pie, in as loud a voice as he can muster, and all at once, Talent will see herself through the eyes of M2YO, not as a failure, or a monster, or even as a human, really, just a physical barrier to pie, and she will temporarily reframe the weekend as a saga about pie, and a 2-year-old's quest to obtain it, and she'll cut him a slice, and watch him shove it in his crusty mouth, stunned by how relieved she is to cede the stage, to give in to somebody— *anybody*—else's demands, and she will laugh out loud for the first time in recent memory, feeling free and for one miraculous moment even slightly thankful.

At any moment, and without prior warning, all terms and conditions are subject to change.

TIME TRAVEL FAMILY COUNSELING INC.

Our company was founded with a simple mission: to allow adult children of baby boomers to send their aging parents to the past in a time machine, so they can show them a traumatic moment from their childhood, and prove once and for all that their version of events is correct.

The first step is to bring your parent in for a consultation. A trained therapist will sit with you while you remind them of their transgression (e.g., the time they blew off your seventh grade clarinet recital). If your parent apologizes, our therapist will congratulate them on their humility and grace. If they say, "That's not how *I* remember it," or accuse you of "exaggerating," or do that fucking look they do sometimes, you know the one I mean, with the weary eyes and the head shake that implies that they're the real victim, because their child is a crazy person who loves to make up lies about them for no reason, then our therapist will taser them unconscious. Once hog-tied, your parent will be strapped inside a Time Orb and blasted at 900 mega gs to the event in question, so they can witness what happened with total objectivity, and the matter can be put to rest, finally, once and for all, after all these fucking years.

Our service is extremely popular, particularly our Day-After-Thanksgiving Package. But before you sign up, we do feel obligated to bring up some caveats. To date, of the 399,372 vindictive adult children who have forced their aging parents to time travel, only 12 percent were "proven right." In the vast majority of cases, the event in question proved to be "more complicated" than they remembered (e.g., while their father did miss the clarinet recital, it was at least partly due to traffic). We are unable to refund your payment in these instances, nor are we able to stop your vindicated parent from gloating, and the grin on their face when they step out of the Time Orb is going to drive you absolutely nuts. Often they've managed to snag one of their favorite discontinued cigarettes while they were in the 1980s, and when they emerge, they light it up in triumph while winking at the therapist, like, "See? What'd I tell you?" I mean, it's the kind of thing that's going to make you just completely lose your mind.

There's another caveat to consider. Even if your

version of events *does* in fact prove to be accurate, there is no guarantee your parent will appreciate the *significance* of their transgression. "It was just a recital," they might say. "It's not like you were performing at Carnegie Hall!" And then they'll laugh and nudge the therapist, trying to get them to join in, and while our therapists are trained to stay impartial, your father's pretty charming when he wants to be, and there's always the possibility he'll win the therapist over to his side, and they'll get all buddy-buddy, and start talking about grilling, and the next thing you know, they're blasting off together in the Time Orb so they can watch Bob Dylan "go electric" at the Newport Folk Festival, and by the time they get back it's the middle of the night and no matter what they say, it's pretty clear that they've been drinking.

The truth is that sending your parent to the past is unlikely to make them see the error of their ways. Physicists refer to this phenomenon as the Boomer Father Paradox, which was originally posited by Austro-Hungarian logician Kurt Gödel, who wrote in a 1931 monograph that "he's never going to fucking change, no matter what. He's just going to keep pulling the same damn shit forever." In layman's terms, what this means is that your parents are incapable of growth. You can spend millions of dollars, rupture space-time, and taser the heck out of them, and they won't learn a thing. It's a foundational law of the universe.

That's why we'd like to make a recommendation.

If you are genuinely interested in using time travel as a tool to repair your relationship with your estranged parent, don't send him back to see your childhood. Instead, send yourself back to see his.

Travel alone to a random day when he was about eight or nine years old. See him walking home from school alone, his chubby legs protruding from his khaki shorts, a soon-to-be outmoded textbook in one hand and a dented *Gunsmoke* lunch box in the other. Watch as two taller boys ride past him on their Schwinns, slapping his buzz-cut head in unison. See the look of terror in his eyes as he tumbles to the sidewalk, then hear his fake laughter as he tries to play the thing off as a joke to a trio of pity-eyed girls. Watch him swallow with panic as he spots the small tear in his shorts. Notice how his pace slows as he trudges toward a small ranch-style house with hideous brown vinyl siding. Fast-forward to dinner and try to follow along as your weirdly jacked grandfather gives a bewildering lecture on manliness, jabbing the air with his fork while your tranquilized grandmother robotically plates chicken à la king. Watch your father hold back tears as he scarfs down a sick bowl of Jell-O, then rushes off for his pathetic bedtime ritual, a murmured plea to God for better days, and then a glance inside a poorly hidden shoebox to make sure his box tops remain, along with his cherished collection of postcards of tap dancers, astronauts, Tahiti, Jacques Cousteau, and a dozen other dreams that died before your birth, before climbing into bed, the metal springs squeaking as he struggles to sleep, two small creases forming underneath his eyes, the precursors to the blotchy, half-moon bags that will someday come to dominate his face. When you can't take it for another second, zap back to the present, where your elderly father sits nervously beside you, wearing glasses he doesn't know are dated and his new favored brand of diabetes socks, which are argyle-patterned to disguise their therapeutic function. Look at his sun-damaged scalp as he bows his head, laughing nervously, holding his breath, waiting for your verdict, hoping you'll absolve him of whatever it is that he did wrong, even though he can't understand or even remember what it was, and ask yourself if it's really unforgivable.

HEY MILLENNIALS

Hey Millennials!

If you've *ever* experienced *any* of these 25 things, then I hate to break the news to you, but you are officially old!

1. The thrill of waking up and seeing that the album you downloaded on Napster is *finally* finished downloading!
2. The joy of discovering a new cheat code in *NBA Jam*!
3. The disgust in your daughter's eyes when she sees your unclothed feet.
4. The fear in her voice when she asks "what happened" to make your feet that way.
5. The indignation of having to explain to her that your feet are not injured or diseased, just affected by the normal processes of age.

6. The humiliation of having to explain to your wife that the reason your daughter is crying is because she's afraid her feet will someday look like yours.

7. The shock of being asked point-blank by your daughter if you are going to die soon, because you are "so old."

8. The reflexive laugh you give when she calls you "old."

9. The observation that your wife, who is slightly younger than you, is not laughing along, and is just kind of staring out into the middle distance with an expression you'd describe as contemplative.

10. The terror of waking up that night from a half-forgotten nightmare, the reality of your own mortality thrumming in your ears, as it hits you like a ton of bricks that your best years are objectively behind you.

11. The determination to stave off this inevitability, no matter what it takes.

12. The pity in your doctor's eyes when you ask her to refer you to a cosmetic podiatrist.

13. The frankness in her voice when she tells you that the main thing for you to focus on right now,

based on your blood work, is not the appearance of your feet but "heart attack prevention."

14. The despair later that week of watching your daughter grab a second hamburger and knowing you can't do the same, because the small one you ate was your full red meat allotment for the month.

15. The sick plop of the veggie burger on your plate.

16. The assessment that your life is like this meal: half finished, with the best half gone.

17. The creeping awareness as you chew your burger that it's not even a veggie burger, but one of those plant-based meat substitute burgers that you've somehow put off trying until now.

18. The confusion of this new meat's flavor, which isn't good, like a hamburger, or bad, like a veggie burger, but something else entirely, something unexpected and profoundly strange. Like...

19. The discovery that someone you considered dumb in high school has become not only rich but respected.

20. The realization that you've been listening to certain bands, reading certain authors, and maintaining certain friendships for decades entirely out of force of habit.

21. The insight that while all your best work will surely be forgotten, your worst work will be, too, so there's no reason not to write that musical about Napoleon.

22. The begrudging acknowledgment that your parents did the best they could, given the circumstances, and that you probably would have done far worse if you'd had to raise children in an era before you could google "toddler when go doctor diarrhea."

23. The exhilarating vision of your daughter's adult life, which you imagine as a vague hybrid of *Mad Max* and the sitcom *Murphy Brown*.

24. The conclusion that the future will be totally beyond your comprehension, by turns shocking, odd, exciting, scary, amazing, and fucked up.

25. The heft of this alien burger, oozing strangely in your hands, as you open your mouth to take another bite.

ACKNOWLEDGMENTS

I want to thank my tireless book agent, Daniel Greenberg, for believing in my writing these past twenty years. Thanks also to my editors at Little, Brown, Michael Szczerban and Khadijah Mitchell; my editors at *The New Yorker,* Susan Morrison and Emma Allen; and my collaborators at the BBC, Jonathan Harvey, Cariad Lloyd, Claire Price, Mat Baynton, Ed Eales-White, Kieran Hodgson, and Adjani Salmon. Additional thanks to Karen Landry, Nell Beram, Alyssa Persons, David Remnick, Lucie Kroening, Daniel Ajootian, Jasper Lo, Lee Eastman, Gregory McKnight, Allan Haldeman, Barrett Festen, Ira Glass, John Mulaney, Conan O'Brien, Ben Stiller, Robert Padnick, Dan Mirk, and all of my therapists. Most of all, I want to thank my wife, Kathleen Hale, who helped me so much with the writing of this book and also with the living that I had to do in order to know how to write it. I love you forever and ever.

ABOUT THE AUTHOR

Simon Rich is a frequent contributor to *The New Yorker.* He is the creator of the TV shows *Man Seeking Woman* and *Miracle Workers,* which he based on his books. His other collections include *Ant Farm, New Teeth,* and *Hits and Misses,* which won the Thurber Prize for American Humor. *Glory Days* is his tenth book.